A New Home

Hartfield Chronicles
Prequel

Ashleigh Stevens

A NEW HOME
First edition. 2022
Copyright © 2022 Ashleigh Stevens

A rewrite of *Boarding School Blues*, 2010, 2018

Print ISBN 978-1-957741-02-4
Ebook ISBN 978-1-957741-01-7

Edited by Work In Progress Wonders
www.WIPWonders.com

Other Works by Ashleigh Stevens

Young Adults
Camp Piquaqua
Elephant on my Chest

Hartfield Chronicles
Lesson 0: A New Home
Lesson 1: Adjusting to a New Life
Webserial

Romances
Kayaks, Kisses & Monsters
Mooncrossed

Mysteries
(writing as Carrie Latimer)
One Night In Sedona

To receive updates on new releases, visit
www.AshleighsStevensBSB.com
or join my newsletter
https://ashleighstevens.eo.page/yanewsletter

A Note from the Author

When I published my debut novel, *Boarding School Blues*, in 2010, I always knew it would become a series. I wanted to follow Melinda's high school journey with a new book each academic term and novellas highlighting each term break.

But I was a new writer and had no idea what I was doing. I inadvertently published the first version of the book through a vanity press. After realizing what had happened, I bought back my rights and republished it through Amazon. I made several minor changes to the second version, mostly correcting some names and typographical errors that I had discovered in the first version.

It took twelve years to create the sequel. During that time, much had changed, especially my writing style. Although I was always proud of my accomplishment, as my writing matured, I noticed more and more flaws in my original story. It felt as if the story followed Melinda's life in excruciating detail with no emotion. There were also entirely too many characters, many with similar names.

By the time the next book was ready for publication, I decided a rebranding was in order just to get some distance from the original story. However, to suggest that Melinda's story begins in *Adjusting to a New Life* would be misleading. I considered sending readers back to the original *Boarding School Blues*, but I have high standards and could not recommend a book that I would not read myself.

So, I created *A New Home*. While most of the story remains true to the original book, I have updated some of the technology (Melinda can now text and video chat with her friends instead of sending instant messages) and altered a handful of names and conversations.

I hope you enjoy following Melinda's journey as much as I enjoy creating it.

Ashleigh Stevens

Chapter 1

IT WAS A TYPICAL FRIDAY NIGHT. UNTIL MY PARENTS delivered the news that would change my life forever.

The evening started like any other. I was in the living room watching a rerun of my favorite science fiction show. The season had ended months ago, but Doc was so cute, I didn't mind seeing it again. Besides, the writers had designed the show in such a way that I saw something new each time I rewatched it.

My parents interrupted me about halfway through the episode, sitting together on the other couch. I was a little confused, since no one in my family had ever shown the slightest interest in *NeoGenesis*. However, when they both turned to face me, I realized they weren't here to watch television.

My mother sighed. "Melinda, we need to talk to you a minute."

I shrugged. "Okay."

"Melinda." My father's tone was grave as he took the remote from the coffee table and turned off the screen. "We need to talk to you about school."

My mother nodded. "I received an email from Mr. Pestle. He said you weren't paying attention in class."

I rolled my eyes. Of course, I wasn't paying attention. Science was so boring. After finishing the classwork in ten minutes, I had pulled out the play we were studying in English class and tried to do the assigned reading. But it wasn't like I was bothering anyone.

Before I could explain this to my parents, however, my father held up a hand. "Your teachers have been emailing us all year, concerned that you spend your class time talking to your friends and not paying attention."

My mother sighed. "We decided to send you to a private school."

I stared at my mother with wide eyes. "What? Just because I was reading in class?"

My mother shook her head. "No, Baby Girl. Because we think you need more of a challenge. You'll learn a lot more at Hartfield than you will if you stay here."

I scoffed. "Yeah, because I'm going to learn so much in the last two weeks of school."

My father smirked. "Hartfield is a high school. You start in September."

High school? My parents wanted to send me to a private high school? To take me away from my friends? Without even asking me? How could they do this to me?

But, I knew having an attitude or yelling at them wouldn't help. If I wanted them to see reason, I had to stay calm. I took a deep breath, looking from my mother to my father and back to my mother.

"What if I don't want to go?"

My father shook his head. "We're not asking your opinion. Your mother and I sent in your application months ago."

My mother nodded. "We received your acceptance letter last week. We were going to wait to discuss it with you, but this email from Mr. Pestle was the third one your teachers have sent this week. It made our decision pretty easy. Next year, you will attend private school."

I was floored. Private school? Was that like military school? I knew nothing about private school. My friends and I all attended public school. So did our siblings. We had all our lives. I didn't know anyone who went to private school.

Except that girl in my tap class. Linda had started a private school a couple of years ago, but she still hung out with her old friends in the afternoons and on the weekends. She hadn't had to quit dancing with us. And she really seemed to enjoy her new school.

Maybe private school wouldn't be such a bad idea after all. My classes *were* pretty uninteresting. Maybe if the work was a little challenging, I would like it more. It wasn't as if I *enjoyed* being so bored at school. I would love to learn new things from my teachers. And I could probably still see my friends after school. We could do homework together. Sure, the assignments would be different, but the company could remain the same.

I was still angry at my parents for making such an important decision without me. But I needed to remain civil with them until I could learn as much about this new place as possible.

I bit my lip. "Maybe private school might be okay."

My mother smiled brightly. "Oh, you're going to love it." Her jollity was nauseating. She passed me the booklet she had been holding in her hand since she entered the room.

I leafed through the brochure. Inside its glossy covers were about ten pages of pictures with very little information. My mother continued her sales pitch.

"It's a wonderful place. Your father and I visited it a couple of months ago. Each subject is in its own building. One for art, one for math, you get the idea. The kids were all very happy. And there's an activities center with video games and TVs and a snack bar."

My father nodded. "There's a brand new athletic center with a fitness room and several gymnasiums. And a dance studio. They offer tons of sports and extracurricular activities."

My mother nodded. "And the rooms were so spacious, too."

I was flipping through the book, only partially paying attention to my rambling parents. What did I care how big the classrooms were? Weren't they all about the same size?

I looked up. "So, where is this Hartfield place?" Maybe I could convince my parents to let me skip school one day to visit it.

My father shrugged. "It's in Oakville."

Even though Connecticut was a small state, we had a lot of towns and I only knew some of their names. I had never heard of Oakville, which meant it probably wasn't nearby. I frowned. "Where is that?"

My mother bit her lip. "In the northeast corner of the state."

I stared at my parents with wide eyes. The northeast corner? We lived on the shoreline, closer to New York than

4

Rhode Island. It would take almost two hours to get to Oakville.

I considered this for a minute. West Shore started around 7:30 in the morning. Assuming this new school did as well, that would mean I would have to leave my house before dawn. I was an early riser, but not that early.

I shook my head. "Not uh. I can't ride a bus two hours, each way, every day!"

My parents glanced at each other before sending me identical sympathetic expressions. I knew that look. It was the one they had shared last year when they told me and my brother that my father was quitting his job to open his own accounting firm. It was the one they shared four years ago when they told us we were moving from our old house into this one. I hated that look.

Before they could share their bad news, the phone rang. My mother nodded toward my father as she rose from the couch. While she went to find the phone in the kitchen, my father sighed.

"Melinda, honey. Hartfield is a boarding school. You don't take the bus there. You live there. If you want, we could visit you every weekend, but—"

He didn't get to finish his sentence. My little brother crashed through the front door. Sure, Joey was eleven years old and in the seventh grade, but I still thought of him as my baby brother. Especially when he was screaming for attention.

Okay. So maybe he *was* covered in mud from head to toe. And I was pretty sure that was blood oozing from his right knee and left elbow.

Well, at least he provided the distraction I needed to run away. While Joey told my father about crashing his bike onto the sidewalk on the dead end road facing our street, I ran upstairs, uncertain if the tears stinging my eyes were anger or sadness.

Locking myself in my room, I searched the internet for information about this Hartfield place. They had a fancy website. Of course they did. They were a private school.

I was awake well past midnight, clicking on every page. In each picture, all the students were smiling. How could they be happy? They *lived* at the *school*.

I could never enjoy myself there. My friends were going to be two hours away from me. I wouldn't see my family, although at the moment, that might be a good thing.

When I realized I was looking at the same pages over and over, I tossed my phone aside and curled up in my bed, crying myself to sleep.

SATURDAY, I SLEPT UNTIL NEARLY ONE IN THE afternoon. That wasn't like me. Unlike other thirteen-year-old girls, I rarely slept in unless I was sick or something. It took a moment to remember the events of the night before.

As much as I wanted to wallow in my bed, I knew I couldn't stay there forever. Brittany's mother would be here soon.

I rolled out of bed, glad my bathroom was in my room. I was in no mood to run into any member of my family this morning.

Taking my time in the shower, I allowed the warm water to envelop me.

I always felt calm in the shower. It helped clear my head and made me feel a little better. I was still upset my parents were sending me away to school, but at least I had finished crying.

Returning to my room, I pulled on some jeans and my favorite purple top before searching for my purse. After tossing in my phone and house key, I checked to see if I had any money in my wallet. Brittany and I were planning to go to the movies, but there was always a chance we might end up grabbing a snack later at one of the many restaurants in the neighboring plazas. After accessorizing with some earrings and a necklace, I opened my bedroom door.

The house was blissfully quiet. I was determined to keep it that way. I had no intention of talking to my parents. Ever again. If they were going to ship me off to boarding school, then they wouldn't hear another word from me. No matter how much they apologized.

I entered the kitchen with a scoff. Like they would ever admit they were wrong. They thought this was a good thing. That boarding school would be great for me. They saw nothing wrong with their decision.

On the kitchen table, I found an empty bowl, a box of cereal, a spoon, and a note, along with two twenty-dollar bills. For a split second, I thought the money was my mother's way of saying she was sorry. That last night had been a prank that had gone too far. I should have known better.

Melinda,

Your father and I are shoping while Joey is at keraty then we are bringing him to the mall. Have fun at the movies. I left you some money. Call us if you need anything.

Mom

My mother's horrible spelling brought a smile to my lips. It tempted me to find a pen to correct it. But my grin quickly faded. I was still mad at my parents. Maybe my mother should go to boarding school instead. She could learn how to spell and I could stay with my friends.

With a sigh, I returned the cereal to the cabinet. It was one of the super sweet sugary ones that Joey liked and I detested. I wasn't much of a breakfast person, anyway. I grabbed some instant oatmeal instead. It wasn't my favorite, and I downed it in a few quick bites. As I was putting my bowl in the dishwasher, the doorbell rang.

Perfect timing.

Chapter 2

WHEN I WAS SIX YEARS OLD, MY TEACHERS AND parents decided I should skip the first grade. On the first day of school, I walked into my second-grade classroom not knowing anyone. Lonely and scared, I headed straight to the desk with my name on it.

Brittany was the first person to greet me that day. She invited me to join her and Casey at the coloring table. The three of us had been inseparable since.

When we were little, we would spend every afternoon at each other's houses, playing dolls and doing crafts. Now, we mostly watched movies and talked about boys. There were no secrets between the three of us.

As I climbed into the car, I was dying to tell Brittany about last night's conversation with my parents. The need to discuss it was churning my stomach. But I didn't want to say anything in front of Brittany's mother. So I let my friend babble about her favorite soap opera instead.

"Can you believe it? Natasha Winters is on *Everly Falls*. And she is so good. I mean, when she cries, I want to cry. She just breaks my heart!"

"Mmm hmm." I wasn't really paying attention, but Brittany seemed satisfied with my response and launched into a summary of yesterday's episode.

The more she yakked, the more annoyed I became. Didn't she realize something was wrong? I was never this quiet. What kind of person was unable to see that her friend was in emotional agony?

I didn't live far from the plaza and Brittany's mother was soon pulling in front of the theater. I climbed out while my friend stuck her head back into the car to make arrangements for when her mother should return. A moment later, she slammed the door. She always slammed the door, but I didn't find it as amusing as I usually did. As her mother pulled away, Brittany spun around and frowned at me.

"Spill it."

Suddenly, I no longer *wanted* to tell her about my new school. I gave a small smile that I didn't wholly feel. "I was wondering how long it would take you to notice something was wrong."

Brittany rolled her eyes. "I knew as soon as you opened your front door. I just knew better than to say something in front of my mom. She's in one of her *I want to be your friend* moods and if she knew something was bothering you, she'd try to fix it. Besides, if it's what I think, I'd get in trouble and I'd rather not get grounded this weekend."

I frowned. "Why would you get in trouble? Umph."

Someone had bumped into me. I glanced around. We *were* kind of blocking the main entrance. People were sending us dirty looks as they tried to enter the theater.

Brittany didn't seem to notice. She shrugged. "Well, I'm assuming your parents are upset about the email Mr. Pestle sent you. I added my mother's email account to my phone, so I deleted it as soon as it came in."

I raised my eyebrows. "You know how to hack into your mother's email?"

My friend rolled her eyes. "It's not like it's hard. She uses the same password for her email as she does for *all* our streaming services. It's her own fault, really."

That still didn't make it right. I was speechless. I had never realized my best friend could be so sneaky. She was always a good girl. When did she start doing things like this?

Brittany was looking at me expectantly. What were we talking about? Oh yeah. I nodded. "Yeah. He emailed my parents."

"And? How long did they ground you? Wait." She glanced around. "If you're grounded, how are you here? Did you sneak out of the house?"

She sounded proud of me. I shook my head slowly. How was I supposed to explain it? I took a deep breath.

"I was sitting on the couch, minding my business, and my parents come in all upset about the email. But they were totally calm about it. And then, they tell me they're going to send me to *private school* next year. I don't have a choice, no matter how hard I complain. And then they tell me it's in

11

Oakville. That's *two hours* from here! And that's when they mention it's a *boarding school* and I'm going to be living there!"

Tears stung my eyes and all the anger I had felt toward my parents last night suddenly returned. When I saw the crushed look on my best friend's face, however, I could no longer rein them in. The floodgates opened, and I bawled right there in the entryway to the movie theater.

Brittany looked dumbfounded. To be fair, if the situation were reversed, I probably wouldn't have known what to say, either.

But when someone bumped into her, she seemed to find her voice. "I don't really feel like a movie anymore, do you?"

I shrugged. I had been looking forward to seeing this movie, but I was so emotionally drained, I wasn't really interested in doing anything at the moment. Besides, I had long ago learned it was easier to go along with my friends than to be more assertive.

The movie theater was nestled in one of four neighboring plazas. I followed Brittany across the parking lot to the nearby bookstore. I wasn't sure if she had chosen it because she knew it was my favorite store or because it was the closest. Or perhaps she just wanted to sit in the café, since she led me directly to that section of the store.

We walked in silence. I had no idea what was going through Brittany's head, but I was thinking about how I would be moving away from my oldest friend. By the time we reached the counter, my sobbing had become a steady stream of tears accompanied by the occasional sniffle. Thankfully, we hadn't run into anyone we knew. The last thing I wanted was to have to explain why I was crying.

I must have masked my despair fairly well because the cheerful cashier didn't seem to notice my distress. She smiled brightly when we reached her.

"Good afternoon. What would you like today?"

Brittany returned the woman's smile. "I'll have a small mocha cappuccino with skim milk. No foam."

The cashier raised her eyebrows. "Are you sure?"

Nodding, Brittany held out some cash. "Definitely."

With a shrug, the woman entered the order into the register, gave my friend her change, and turned to the hissing machine.

I was in shock. Since when did Brittany drink coffee? She was barely fourteen. Coffee was for grownups.

I tapped her shoulder, whispering so the woman behind the counter wouldn't hear me. "Are you sure about this?"

"Yeah. You want to try some? It is so good. It's like a really creamy hot chocolate."

I raised my eyebrows. "You've had one before?"

"Sure. It's my mom's favorite drink. I've shared it with her loads of times."

Unconvinced, I scanned the café while we were waiting for Brittany's drink. I had a suspicion she had ordered coffee to impress someone. Not that it would make a difference. They served all the drinks in the same white paper cups with brown lids.

But I didn't see anyone. There was a college-aged girl reading a book while eating a scone. When I saw her put it down to run a highlighter along a couple of lines, I was horrified. Didn't her teachers ever tell her not to make any marks in the book?

Shuddering, I glanced at the table beside her. A man about the same age as my father sat with a boy a little younger than my brother. The man was trying to read a magazine with a motorcycle on the cover, but he was constantly returning it to the table in order to answer the boy's questions about the book he was reading. I couldn't hear their conversation, but the man looked exasperated.

At the only other occupied table sat a boy surrounded by stacks of books and magazines. They all seemed to be about video games. Besides his paper cup, he also had a plate with half a giant chocolate chip cookie.

"What can I get for you, sweetie?"

I turned around. Brittany was sipping her drink, and the cashier was looking at me expectantly. I bit my lip. I wanted to appear as sophisticated as my friend, but I had sipped my mother's coffee, too. It was disgusting.

The café served hot chocolate. That was probably a safe drink, even if it was June and nearly seventy degrees outside.

After paying for my beverage, I looked at my friend for her approval. But her attention wasn't on me. She was staring at the video game boy. I glanced at his table.

He was no longer reading, but returning Brittany's gaze with a shy smile. I recognized him immediately, of course. Geeky Greg was in all my classes this year. Except specials. At least I got that ninety-minute break from him each day.

And man, did I need it. Geeky Greg was super annoying and extremely hyper, always talking about video games so rapidly, I sometimes wondered if he was still speaking English. He had a few friends, but not many. Most of our class didn't like him, though the majority of us could tolerate him, at least during the school day.

But why was Brittany smiling at him?

"Here's your drink, sweetie."

With a start, I turned. I had forgotten where we were. I reached for my cup. "Thanks."

Before I could take a sip, Brittany grabbed my free arm. "Let's go sit with Greg."

Why? Wasn't spending five hours a day with him enough? Why would I join him on the weekend?

This was probably one of those things I would never understand. Like that summer before middle school, when I wanted to play house and my friends declared they would rather read teen magazines and plan their perfect dates. Even though none of us *were* teens or even allowed to have boyfriends.

With a sigh, I let Brittany drag me to Geeky Greg's table. He looked as surprised as I felt. She gave a small giggle as we approached.

"Hi, Greg. Can we join you?"

His face lit up. "Yeah. Sure. Of course. Lemme just—"

He moved the stack of books onto the empty chair beside him. My friend settled herself across from him. Unsure what else to do, I sat gingerly beside her.

Brittany took a sip of her coffee. "So, whatcha up to?" Her manner was so nonchalant, as if we had always been friends with Geeky Greg and it was completely normal to be sitting with him in a bookstore café on the weekend.

Geeky Greg shrugged. "N-not much." His voice was a little squeaky. He sipped his drink, then gestured to the book in front of him. "I'm trying to find a cheat code so I can get past the Demon Lord in the ninth level of *Arch Enemy*."

"Wow. You're already at the ninth level?"

Brittany sounded impressed. I was clueless. I had never heard of *Arch Enemy*, although I assumed it was some sort of video game. How many levels were there? Was being at the ninth one good or bad?

And why did I even care?

Geeky Greg shrugged. "It wasn't that hard. But the Demon Lord is really difficult to get past."

He launched into a detailed description involving magic potions, fireproof boots, and guardian dragons. I had no clue what he was saying and, frankly, didn't really care. But Brittany was nodding, hanging on his every word. When he took a sip of his drink, she pointed to the stack of books.

"Want us to help you look?"

Seriously? She had understood that ramble? And was she really volunteering me, too?

Geeky Greg's face lit up. "Sure."

He grabbed a book from the pile beside him and slid it across the table. As he explained to Brittany some keywords that would aid her search, I grew uncomfortable. I was feeling like I didn't belong here.

I gestured over my shoulder. "I'm just going to go find that book I was telling you about."

Brittany didn't respond. She was too absorbed with Geeky Greg.

As I walked away from the table, my heart broke again. I was losing my best friend. This morning, I had assumed it was because of that stupid boarding school. But now it looked like I was losing her to Geeky Greg. When did that *happen*? And why didn't Brittany tell me about it?

16

Chapter 3

I WANDERED AIMLESSLY THROUGH THE ROWS OF books with only two things on my mind: Brittany's behavior and boarding school. Since I was pretty sure I wouldn't find any books about my friend, I decided to research my new school. Sure, all those pictures last night made it *seem* like everyone was happy. But maybe there was a book that would tell me how horrible it really was. I would leave it by my parents' bed. Maybe they would change their mind about sending me.

Sighing, I looked at the books surrounding me. I was in the science fiction section. Yeah, my life felt like it was becoming some scary sci-fi novel, but I doubted I would find anything describing Hartfield here. Which section had the books about *schools where parents send kids when they want to ruin their lives?*

I went to the customer service desk. The older man behind the counter smiled at me.

"Hi. Can I help you find something?"

I nodded. "Yeah. I was wondering if you had any books about private schools."

The man smiled. "We have lots. Can you give me a little more information? Are you looking for novels? Or non-fiction?"

I shrugged. "Nonfiction, I guess. I'm trying to find information about a specific boarding school."

The man nodded. "Those would be in our college section." He typed something into his computer. "Aisle 28. Would you like me to show you?"

"No, thank you. I can find it. Thanks."

With a small wave, I walked away, glancing at the signs on the side of each row. It wasn't difficult to find number twenty-eight. The hard part was selecting the right book.

Most of the them were about colleges. But two-thirds down the aisle, I found a section with books about private elementary and high schools. Since it was near the bottom of the shelf, I had no qualms plopping myself onto the floor right in front of it.

I wasn't really sure what to look for, but scanned the titles before me. *Private Schools in Connecticut* caught my eye. Glancing at the copyright page, I learned the book was only a year old. Perfect. The information would be up to date.

I flipped to the index, finding Hartfield easily. When I turned to the suggested page, I discovered a brief history of the school. Unfortunately, I didn't read far before getting lost. With a sigh, I pulled out my phone and opened my dictionary app, then tried again.

Charles Hartfield founded the Charles Hartfield School for Young Men in 1873 with a population of fifteen students. Located on eighteen acres in the quiet northeastern corner of Connecticut, the school comprised three edifices. The primary building contained two classrooms, separating the upper and lower school students. A chapel held services for the boys every Sunday. The third building was a dormitory to house all fifteen boys, as well as Hartfield and his wife.

Rachel Hartfield served as the housekeeper and chef for her husband's school until 1898, when she decided young ladies needed their own learning institution. By this time, Hartfield's original school had grown and the demand for new buildings was too large to ignore. After the construction of three new dormitories, two classroom buildings, and a dining hall, Mrs. Hartfield opened her school to a score of girls.

In 1974, the two schools merged to become a single coeducational facility, now known as the Charles and Rachel Hartfield Preparatory Academy for Young Men and Women. Over the years, the school has gained a very prestigious reputation and has been home to many celebrities and their children.

The rest of the page was more or less a list of some of the school's most famous former students. I closed the book with a sigh. My parents were basically sending me to a fancy, popular school where people went to class in one building, ate in another, and slept in a third.

I couldn't be any less excited.

I spent the next half hour glancing through the other books in the section, but if they mentioned Hartfield, it was only to give me similar information. Nothing I read gave me any clue about the whole boarding school experience.

What would it be like to live in a dormitory? Would I get used to saying the word? How was I supposed to make new friends when I had been with the same classmates since the second grade? Would I be able to keep in touch with Brittany and Casey, even though I would live two hours away? Even if I was already losing one of them to the geekiest boy in school and I hadn't even left yet?

I could feel the tears threatening again. I no longer wanted to be sitting alone in the bookstore. Even though no one was around, it felt like everyone was looking at me. I needed to get out of here.

As I rushed toward the front door, I glanced at the café. What I really needed was a hug from my best friend. But, she was sitting with Geeky Greg talking about stupid video games.

I caught sight of her as I passed. The stack of books was back on the table and Brittany had moved into the seat beside him. The two of them were laughing. Eww.

Outside, I sat on a bench and took a few deep breaths. I wasn't sure what to do next. It would be several hours before Brittany's mother returned. My own parents were an hour away. Not that I was in the mood to talk to them, either.

In a way, however, Brittany had helped me. I was so angry at her, I no longer wanted to cry. Walking off the anger sounded like a much better idea.

Making my way along the plaza, I headed to the neighboring beauty supply store. Last week at lunch, Casey had shown me her new favorite nail polish. Maybe buying some would make me feel better.

I was so busy trying to remember the name that I wasn't paying attention to where I was going. As I approached the store, the door opened, and I nearly bumped into the person leaving.

I looked down quickly. "I'm sorry."

"Melinda?"

I glanced up at the familiar voice. I couldn't quite read the expression on Casey's mother's face. Was she concerned or amused? Maybe a little of both?

I bit my lip. "Oh. Hi."

She smiled. "Hey, sweetie. How are you? Are you here with your mother?"

I shook my head. "No. Brittany and I were at the bookstore and I remembered I wanted to come here for a minute."

As soon as the words were out of my mouth, I felt guilty. What if Casey's mother went next door and saw Brittany talking to Geeky Greg? She would tell Brittany's mother, who would ground my friend for life. The last time I checked, our moms still thought we were too young to have boyfriends.

At the same time, I felt guilty about being out with Brittany and not Casey. Why *hadn't* we invited her? The three of us were usually inseparable. Would her mother think we had slighted her?

Casey's mother smiled. "Yes, Casey told me you two were out today. But I thought she said you were at the movies."

I nodded slowly. "We were. I mean, we were going to go, but we changed our minds when we got there."

"Casey wanted to join you, but she had her piano lessons. She's next door buying a new leash for Trixie."

"Do you think maybe she can spend the day with me and Brittany? Brittany's mom's picking us up around 5:30. I'm sure she can bring Casey home, too."

Her mother nodded. "I don't see why not."

I smiled for the first time all day. "Great! I'll go tell her. Thanks!" Forgetting about the nail polish, I continued along the plaza to the pet store.

Even though the place was enormous, I had a good idea where to find my best friend. I didn't own any pets, but I knew the store like the back of my hand. Casey had dragged me there often enough.

Casey's parents had bought a toy poodle not long before I had met her. Although Trixie was technically the family's dog, she and Casey had a special bond. She loved to pamper the dog with treats and toys. She could easily spend hours searching for the perfect pink leash for the small dog.

However, I found her in an aisle of chew toys. Silently, I snuck behind her.

"Boo!"

Screaming, Casey jumped and turned around, smiling when she saw me. "What're you doing here? Aren't you supposed to be eating popcorn and watching Jarrod Handy right now?"

"Change of plans. First of all, I ran into your mom and she said you can spend the day with me and Brittany."

Casey looked around. "Where *is* Britty?"

I rolled my eyes. "So, we skipped the movie—I'll tell you about that in a sec—and we ended up at the bookstore café. You'll never guess what Brittany ordered."

Casey frowned. "That coffee her mom drinks?"

I pouted. "You know her too well. Anyway, I bet you'll never guess who she's sitting with right now."

"Well, I'd guess you, but you're here, so I'm clueless."

I lowered my voice to a conspiratorial whisper. "Geeky Greg!"

Casey's eyes went wide. "Really? Oh, I got to see this!"

I followed my friend to the register, where she paid for Trixie's new leash and toys. As we headed back to the bookstore, she sent me a confused look.

"So, why didn't you guys go to the movie?"

I sighed. "I was too upset to enjoy a movie. Last night, my parents got an email from Mr. Pestle that I was disturbing class and they decided that they're going to send me to *boarding school* next year. Can you believe it? It's *two hours* away. I'm going to have to *live* there!"

"They're *what*?"

I nodded. "Yup. And then, when I tried to tell Brittany about it, she completely abandoned me to go talk to Geeky Greg, of all people."

Casey put an arm around my shoulders, pulling me into a slight hug. "You poor thing. We should totally go bust in on Brittany."

As we neared the café, however, I couldn't do it. My friend looked so happy to be spending time with a boy. I turned to Casey.

"Let's leave Brittany alone."

Casey shrugged. "But we can sit in the café and make fun of her, right?"

I smiled. "Totally."

Grabbing a handful of magazines, we settled into some chairs just outside the café area. As we flipped through the pages, Casey suddenly remembered about her cousin in Long Island.

"She goes to this all-girls school."

I shook my head. "Hartfield is, what was the word? I forgot. But I remember it meant it had boys and girls."

Out of the corner of my eye, I saw Greg leaving the table. As Brittany made her way toward us, Casey gave a sigh of relief.

"Oh, that's good. I would go nuts if there were no boys. I don't know how my cousin does it. Do you have to wear a uniform? She's got this ugly plaid skirt and a horrible blouse. Oh, and this funky little tie thing."

I winced. "Gah, I hope not." I tried to remember the images I had seen on the school website. "I don't think there are uniforms."

Brittany's eyes went wide as she looked at me. "Oh, Melinda! I am *soooo* sorry. I completely forgot. The second I saw Greg, he was all I could think about. I never meant to abandon you like that!"

I giggled. "Britty, it's okay." I motioned for her to sit with me, and she squeezed into my oversized chair. Talking to Casey had helped me get rid of a lot of the hurt and anger that my parents had generated last night and Brittany had fueled this afternoon. I was still mad at my parents for sending me away, but I wasn't mad at my friend. Especially since she had just apologized.

Brittany put her arm around me. "Seriously? I'm forgiven?"

I rolled my eyes. "Of course."

Brittany frowned. "You're not gonna, like, tell my parents just to get even, right?"

It hurt that she would think me capable. Of course, I could never do that.

Before I could respond, however, Casey shook her head. "Brit! You know Melly would *never* do that! You're just lucky I was here to be a better friend. Because otherwise, when I found out, I might tell your mom."

I could see Brittany trying to be mad, but she couldn't help but laugh. I bumped my shoulder against hers.

"So, care to explain why you ditched me for Geeky Greg?"

Brittany frowned. "Don't call him that! He's not that bad."

Casey smirked. "He's obsessed with video games."

"Yeah, I know, but it's kind of cute."

"So, is he your boyfriend now?"

I looked between my two friends. Boyfriend? How did that happen? Sure, my friends enjoyed talking about boys, but I thought Brittany was just talking to Geeky Greg. Boyfriend seemed to be a big step.

Beside me, Brittany nodded excitedly. Casey squealed. I was still dumbfounded. I managed a small smile and tried to be happy for my friend. But inside, part of me was sad.

I was losing my best friend. I may have been new to all this, but I was pretty sure that having her having a boyfriend was going to change things between us. And then I would be leaving for school. Would anything stay the same?

Chapter 4

THE REST OF JUNE WENT BY SO QUICKLY, I HARDLY realized time was passing. Finally, the last week of school arrived. My classmates ran around, signing each other's yearbooks in lunch and homeroom. Brittany took mine for her entire math class. Casey brought it home overnight while she thought of the perfect message.

Around me, my friends and classmates seemed to discuss nothing but high school. Everyone was excited because they would be the first freshman class in the new building.

"After all," one of my classmates explained with a smile, "that means we won't be the only people wandering the halls in a daze on the first day. Even the teachers will be lost."

All the high school talk made me crave more information about Hartfield. But, I knew very little. And not even my parents could tell me anything new. They kept saying I would have to wait.

Because of a multitude of snow days this year, school dragged on until the last week of June. I sat in stifling hot classrooms that lacked air conditioning, dying of heat while my teachers tried to cram in some last-minute lessons that went in one ear and out the other. None of my classmates, not even Geeky Greg or his nerdy friends, paid them any attention.

It was nearly July when we finally reached the last day of school. As the end of day bell approached, my classmates all hugged each other with wishes of a wonderful summer. I, however, felt as if I were saying goodbye forever. And it stung.

When the day was finally over, my classmates ran through the halls, throwing loose papers. It was a long-standing tradition my parents remembered from their own junior high days.

Somehow, I couldn't picture my new prim and proper private school classmates doing the same thing. They probably spent summers crying that classes were over. It wouldn't surprise me if they saved all their notes to review during the summer vacation to get ahead.

I was halfway to the bus when I remembered my mother was supposed to be picking me up. It only occurred to me when I saw Brittany and Casey waiting for me in front of the main entrance. I couldn't believe I had forgotten. We had only spent *all day* talking about it.

My friends and I piled into the backseat of my mother's SUV with me in the middle. Brittany and Casey chattered animatedly over me during the short drive to the shopping plaza. But, I couldn't join in their conversation.

I couldn't stop thinking about how different my life was going to be. Even though we would all be in new schools next year, they would be in classes with people they had known since kindergarten. They wouldn't need to make new friends.

As my mother pulled in front of the bookstore, I saw Geeky Greg getting out of a car a few stores away. I tried not to roll my eyes. Even though he and Brittany had been together for a few weeks, I had not gotten used to him being around. And it was incredibly difficult for me to think of him as just plain *Greg*.

I waited until my mother had pulled away from the curb before turning to Brittany. "Is Gee—uh, Greg—joining us?"

Casey wrinkled her nose in my direction. "How do you not know this? We're meeting up with Greg and a couple of his friends at the new diner. We've been planning this all week."

I had certainly not known about this. As much as I loved my friends, I probably wouldn't have come if I *had* known. I was pretty sure I knew who would join us for lunch. Geeky Greg's two best friends were Nick and Eliot. Sure, I had been nursing crushes on both boys last month, but neither was serious. I had nearly every class with both boys and Nick had grown increasingly more annoying over the past few weeks.

Eliot, at least, I could tolerate. Since Brittany had unofficially swapped seats with him over the last few weeks, we had been chatting a lot during geography and science.

Although we had all known each other forever, I couldn't recall ever spending time with the boys outside of school. Except, maybe, church and the religious education classes Brittany, Eliot, and I had shared. But that wasn't any different from school.

I looked around as we waited to cross the street. "I haven't been to the diner yet. Is it any good?"

Nick nodded. "Yeah, my brother's been working there since they opened back in, what? March? I've been a few times. It's not Charley's, but it's not bad."

I nodded. Charley's was everyone's favorite diner and was always packed on the weekends. Although no one ever talked about this new place like the other diner, every time I passed it, the lot looked full.

Thankfully, though, not at the moment. We had no problems getting a booth for six.

I had assumed we would sit with the boys facing us. Casey slid into one seat and Nick climbed in across from her. Brittany sat on the girls' side and Eliot followed his friend. But Greg was in front of me and squeezed in beside his girlfriend before I could.

Biting my lip, I gingerly took the seat beside Eliot, trying to keep as much space between us as possible. I had never been this close to him—or any boy, really.

To make matters worse, I couldn't talk to my friends without leaning over Eliot. Not that it was a problem, since Brittany and Geeky Greg were whispering to each other and Casey was too busy talking to Nick to notice me.

Even though I knew I wanted grilled cheese, I stared at my menu, hoping I didn't look as uncomfortable as I felt. After the server took my order—and menu—I realized I would have to have a conversation with Eliot. Somehow, even though it was so easy to talk to him in class, I had no idea what to say now.

He broke the silence. "So, you think we'll still be in the same homeroom next year?"

I shook my head. "No. I'm, uh, I'm not going to West Shore next year."

He frowned. "You're not?"

I bit my lip. The last thing I wanted was for Eliot to think I was bragging about my new school, but I also didn't want it to seem like I was looking for his pity, either.

I sighed. "No. My parents are sending me to a private school instead."

A few months ago, we had reenacted a play in English class. Eliot had performed the role of a father who had just lost his son. The look on his face now matched the one he had worn in that scene. I quickly tried to explain myself.

"My parents thought I was bored in class and needed more of a challenge, so they're sending me to this place out in Oakville. It's a boarding school."

Eliot's face brightened. "Hey, I know where that is! My uncle lives in Oakville. I didn't realize there was a boarding school there. Is it nice?"

I shrugged. "I haven't been there. But, I looked online, and it doesn't look so bad. But, still. It's not here. I won't know anyone."

Eliot nodded, but he didn't seem to know what to say next. I was certainly clueless. Our awkward silence grew increasingly more uncomfortable, making it that much harder to think about what to say.

Thankfully, the server arrived with our food. All conversation stopped as we passed around condiments. The boys had gotten burgers, but Brittany and Casey looked slightly disgusted that I had ordered a grilled cheese instead of a salad like they had.

It didn't take long for everyone else to resume their conversations, and an awkward silence again fell between me and Eliot. After a few bites, he nodded in my direction.

"So, you doing anything exciting over the summer? You know, before you get shipped to some shunk place you don't even want to go?"

I didn't reply immediately. I was in too much shock. Had Eliot really just said *shunk*? Only a genuine fan of *NeoGenesis* would know the swear used abundantly throughout the show.

But I knew better than to ask him outright. If I was wrong, he and his friends might tease me like the seventh grader on my bus that had been taunted mercilessly after accidentally admitting he was a shunkhead.

Then again, today was probably the last time I would ever see these boys. So, it didn't really matter if he made fun of me.

I took a sip of soda to help bolster my confidence. "Um, no. No plans. Eliot, did you say *shunk*?"

Eliot was notorious for turning red when he was embarrassed. Our classmates used to prank him in elementary school just to see his reaction. Yet, in all the years I had known him, I had never seen him turn such a deep shade of red as he was becoming now. His burger seemed to be the most interesting thing in the room, since he wouldn't meet my eye.

Finally, he responded in a barely audible whisper. "Uh, yeah. It's from a television show my dad watches."

I smirked. "Yeah, but only a true shunkhead would actually say it."

Eliot's dumbfounded expression was so comical, I burst out laughing. Everyone turned to me. While my friends shot me dirty looks, probably annoyed that I had interrupted their conversations, the boys both seemed disappointed they had missed the joke.

Geeky Greg looked between me and Eliot a few times. "What's so funny?"

While Eliot just shook his head, I took a sip of soda to help me catch my breath before responding. "Inside joke."

31

My friends' expressions immediately changed. I knew from their smirks that they were pleased Eliot and I had shared something private. They probably thought I was flirting. Although I wanted to correct them, I wasn't about to share the real secret with them. They would likely make fun of me, getting the other boys to join in.

I didn't need to worry, though. As soon as they realized I wasn't doing anything to embarrass them, they went back to their conversations. I smiled at Eliot.

"It's cool that you watch NG. I've never met anyone our age who does. Well, except for this kid on my bus. But he made the mistake of telling someone he was a shunkhead and now everyone makes fun of him."

Eliot pointed at me. "Oh! I think I know the guy you mean. Isn't he in band with us?"

"Yup. So, you watch the show with your dad?"

"Yeah. You know this is a remake, right?"

I sipped my soda with a nod.

"Well, he was a hug fan of the original show back when he was our age. So, he was really excited about the new one. I watched the pilot with him and was hooked."

"That's cool. I just kind of stumbled on it one day. Fell in love with it." And the cute doctor, though I would never admit that to Eliot.

He and I spent the rest of the meal comparing some of our favorite *NeoGenesis* episodes. After lunch, we wandered through the plaza with our friends, and it was a lot easier to talk to him. Which was a good thing, since everyone else was too busy paying attention to each other to spare us a glance.

I didn't say anything, but I couldn't help noticing Casey's fingers entwined with Nick's. It baffled me how she could want to be with someone so irritating. First Geeky Greg and now Annoying Nick? What was happening to my friends?

When Nick's older brother arrived, Casey went to greet him while Greg whispered to Brittany. Biting my lip, I turned to Eliot. Why wasn't he getting in the car? He looked like he wanted to say something, but words seemed to have escaped him.

Finally, Greg kissed Brittany—on the cheek—and climbed into the car. Eliot gave me a small wave, mumbled something that might have been *goodbye*, and slid in beside him. After Nick squeezed Casey's hand, he got in the front seat and closed the door, waving as his brother pulled away from the curb.

It surprised me that I was so sad. I wasn't sure I was ever going to see these boys again. I wouldn't miss them or anything, but there was something about the finality of this goodbye that made me mournful.

My friends and I continued our wanderings, window shopping and even trying on some clothes in the boutiques, until we finally found ourselves at the bookstore. We were lounging on the couches, reading magazines, when Casey's mother arrived.

On the way back to Casey's house, we picked up pizza, which her mother let us bring upstairs. Brittany and I found our overnight bags waiting for us in Casey's room. We had packed them last night and our mothers had brought them while we were in school.

I nodded toward the door as we settled ourselves on the floor. "Hey Case? Where's the rest of your family? It's so quiet."

Casey rolled her eyes. "Kevin's at T-ball with my dad. Trish is out with her boyfriend."

"And Gracie?"

Casey shrugged. "One of her friends invited her over. My mom said she'd make sure she doesn't bother us when she gets home."

I nodded politely as I bit into my pizza. I wouldn't have minded Gracie joining us. Even though she was only a few years younger than us, an illness as an infant had left her with some severe delays in her emotional and intellectual development. Yet, she was the sweetest girl I knew and gave some of the best hugs. I loved her like she was my own sibling.

But I knew Casey wouldn't tolerate her little sister tonight. She and Brittany just wanted to talk about spending the afternoon with the Nick and Greg. As if texting them between bites of pizza wasn't enough. They had to analyze everything the boys were saying.

A little while later, Casey squealed when her phone signaled a request for a video chat. Rolling my eyes, I watched as Casey took a few calming breaths and accepted the call.

"Hey."

Casey angled the phone so that Brittany and I could see the screen, although Nick could only see her. He smiled.

"Hey. I had a great time today."

Casey smiled. "Yeah. Me, too."

"So, I was thinking. Maybe we could do it again sometime. Hang out."

Casey shrugged. "I would like that."

"And maybe you would like to be my girlfriend?"

Brittany squeezed my arm so hard, I thought I was going to lose circulation in my fingers. She had rolled her lips inward and was obviously trying not to shriek in excitement. I did my best to focus my attention back on the screen.

Casey nodded. "Yeah. Of course."

While she went into a corner to talk to Nick with a little more privacy, Brittany's phone rang. Squealing, she moved to another corner to whisper with Geeky Greg.

I wanted to be happy for my friends. They both had boyfriends and were really excited about it. But, I felt a little lonely as I settled on Casey's bed, watching random internet videos on my phone while I waited for my friends.

It took awhile, but eventually Brittany and Casey ended their calls and decided we should watch some movies. We moved to the living room so we could stream on the big screen. The first movie was so scary, I was positive I would have nightmares. After pulling out the sofa bed, we settled on a sappy romance to help chase away the potential bad dreams.

A little after midnight, when we were all sobbing over the boyfriend's death, Trisha waltzed through the door. Casey waved to her older sister as she passed us.

"Hey, Trish. How was your date?"

Her sister sat on the edge of the bed. "Not bad. We went to the movies."

Brittany smirked. "Did he kiss you?"

Trisha scoffed. "Like I would tell you." She nodded toward the screen. "Whatcha watching?"

"Bridesmaids in Love. Are you and Trevor in love?"

Trisha got to her feet with a sigh. "Night, girls."

Casey was asleep before the end of the movie. After the happily ever after, Brittany turned off the television and was soon snoring. But, I couldn't sleep.

Staring at the ceiling, I couldn't help but feel a little mournful. Today had been my last day of public school, probably forever. I had assumed I would spend the summer with my friends, but now I wasn't so sure. Brittany and Casey both had boyfriends. Would they want to hang out with me or them over the next few months?

Would this be our last summer together? Was Hartfield going to change our friendship? What would happen to the three musketeers?

Chapter 5

I WASN'T SURE WHEN I FELL ASLEEP, BUT I WAS THE first of my friends awake in the morning. My internal clock wouldn't let me sleep past nine. Knowing I had a while before my friends woke, I pulled out my phone and called up the website where I had been spending most of my time lately. Hartfield's website.

I had clicked on all the links more times than I could count. Nothing was new since my last visit yesterday morning. They hadn't even changed their *Daily Docket*, the school's daily newsletter, since the beginning of the month. After something called *commencement*, there had been no more updates.

I was trying to figure out where to click next when my phone signaled a video chat request from an unknown caller. When I denied it, I received a text from the same number. *It's Eliot.* He followed the message with a *NeoGenesis* gif. Smiling, I sent a video request, and he answered immediately.

"Hey. You're up early."

I raised my eyebrows. "You texted me."

He shrugged. "I didn't think you'd actually answer."

I rolled my eyes. "Why you awake?"

"Firetrucks across the street woke me up."

I gasped. "Everyone okay?"

"Yeah. It was a false alarm."

"Sorry it woke you up."

Eliot shrugged again. "I didn't mind. I was going to keep reading this new book I bought last week, but I decided to re-watch *NG* from the beginning instead. See how many Easter eggs I could find."

I gasped. "That is *such* a good idea. That is so how I am going to spend my summer!"

I was serious. One of the best parts about *NeoGenesis* was finding clues in early episodes that helped predict the surprises later in the season. I had spent the first few weeks viewing online videos that identified most of them, but between dance and school, I had eventually forgotten about them. Binge watching them sounded like a great way to spend my summer.

Eliot and I compared some of our favorite fan sites for a while. When he mentioned my new school, I sent him the link to the Hartfield website. When I asked what book he was reading, he told me about his favorite author and described the legal thriller series. He was wide-eyed when I shared that I had been reading the *NeoGenesis* novels written when the original series was popular.

I nodded. "Yeah. Our library has the entire collection. I plan on re-reading it this summer, too."

Eliot smirked. "Not if I check them all out first." He glanced over his shoulder before turning back to me. "Hey. It's getting kind of late. My father and I are heading out in a little while. I better get ready."

I gave a small wave. "Have fun."

As I ended the call, I glanced over at my friends. They were still out cold. With a sigh, I dug through my bag for the novel I had gotten from the library the other day. Eliot couldn't check out the entire *NeoGenesis* series. I already had.

With a smile, I moved to the floor to give myself a little more room, resting on my stomach as I became absorbed in a futuristic world full of spaceships and cute doctors. I never heard my friends stirring. I only knew they were awake because Casey stepped on my butt.

"Morning, bookworm."

I looked up to see her smiling down at me.

"Want breakfast?"

My friends spent most of the day texting their boyfriends, although I managed to convince them to take a short walk around the neighborhood. Brittany suggested we go the few blocks to her house to go swimming, but Casey's mother refused to let us near the pool with no adult at home.

My mother picked me up a few hours before dinner, dropping Brittany at her house on our way home. At the bottom of our driveway, my mother stopped the car.

"Can you grab the mail, Baby Girl?"

Rolling my eyes, I climbed out of the car. The box was stuffed. I flipped through the letters as I followed the car to the garage. Random catalogs for my mother from companies I didn't recognize. Junk mail for my father from state and national accounting associations. A few credit card offers for me and my younger brother. A handful of bills. A large, thick envelope that probably had some sort of software for my father. Two letters from the Mapledale Public School system. Our report cards.

I went through the garage, grabbing my bag from the car before entering the house. I nearly froze as I crossed the threshold. Outside was almost tropical. Someone had set the air conditioning inside to igloo.

Placing the pile of mail on the table, I opened my report card. I had a B in gym, but that didn't surprise me. I was a dancer, not an athlete, and never gave that class my best effort. The rest of my teachers had given me A's, although each of them mentioned me talking out of turn and disturbing the class.

That was so not true. I wasn't a disturbance. I was just talking to my friends when I was bored. Sure, sometimes my teachers said I was being a little loud. But, I usually would stop talking when my teacher looked at me. For a few minutes, anyway.

My mother reappeared in the kitchen, nodding toward the paper in my hand. "Anything interesting?"

Shrugging, I held out the page. "Report card."

My mother pursed her lips as she read through the comments, but she said nothing. Instead, she turned to the pile on the table. The thick envelope immediately caught her eye. I pointed to the label.

"Hey. That's addressed to me!"

My mother already had it in her hands, opening the envelope and removing its contents: a glossy black folder and a small paperback. Passing me the book, she skimmed through the folder, taking a couple of sheets of paper.

"Hmm. I'm going to need to stop by your doctor to get these forms filled out. I don't think you'll need another physical, though." She handed me the folder. "You can read through the rest of this."

I didn't want to. I'd rather throw it all away and pretend I wasn't going to a new school. But maybe these pages would answer some of my questions about Hartfield.

I stomped up to my bedroom, tossing my overnight bag near my door beside the backpack my mother must have placed there last night. Flopping onto my stomach on my bed, I leafed through the folder first.

The letter on top was again congratulating me on my acceptance to Hartfield. I didn't think congratulations were in order. They should apologize that I was being sent there against my will. The letter continued, listing the contents of the folder and what to do with them. The first ones were the medical history and immunization forms. Unfortunately, I had no idea what that meant.

With a sigh, I rolled off my bed, digging through my desk for an unused composition book. I knew I had an extra one somewhere. I found it at the bottom of the biggest drawer. After grabbing a pen, I used my fanciest handwriting to write *Melinda's Vocabulary Journal* on the front cover.

Back in sixth grade, my English teacher had assigned us to have a notebook to record unfamiliar words, writing the definitions in our own terms to help us learn them. Unlike my classmates, I had continued the journal through seventh and eighth grade. It was still in my backpack, although I was getting close to the last page.

But I was starting high school, and it only made sense to begin a new journal. I thought about all the unfamiliar words I had encountered since my parents first mentioned Hartfield. *Dormitory. Comprise. Edifice. Score. Prestigious. Co-educational. Commencement.* Although I remembered the words, I had to search for each definition again. After entering them into my new journal, I looked up *immunization,* only to learn that the form my doctor had to fill out was the list of vaccines I had received since I was born.

I left my journal open beside me as I returned my attention to the folder. I was pretty sure my mother had taken the medical forms. The next page was the schedule for *orientation* weekend. With a sigh, I added that word to my journal. The paper supposedly listed all the meetings and events that would help me adjust to my new home. I wasn't sure how a few gatherings would make it easier to adapt to such a humongous change, but I still searched for the page, placing it beside me on the bed. I would read it in a moment.

Behind it was a list of items allowed and forbidden within the dorms. There were so many things banned, I felt as if nothing was permitted. Then again, I wasn't even sure how some items had made it onto the list in the first place. Seriously, why would anyone bring fireworks or weapons to school in the first place? And what exactly was a *vape pen*?

Televisions weren't allowed, but I wasn't too concerned. I would just have to stream my favorite shows on my computer. I was more upset that I was forbidden to bring the scented candles I loved to burn while I was studying. Yeah, I could see where they might cause a fire hazard or something, but it was still very disappointing.

With a sigh of frustration, I turned back to the letter. The final paragraph instructed me to read through the school handbook, using the QR code at the end to acknowledge that I had done so. Maybe if I didn't sign it, I wouldn't have to attend?

The signature at the bottom of the page belonged to the *headmaster*, who I quickly learned was the person in charge of Hartfield. I wasn't exactly sure if he was the private school version of a principal or superintendent, but he was definitely the head honcho.

After adding that word to my vocabulary journal, I skimmed the handbook. About the size of a paperback, it was almost a hundred pages long. Although it started friendly enough, discussing the school's mission statement and other boring information, it was ultimately a book of rules, along with very detailed explanations of what would happen if students were to break each one.

And there were rules for everything. Rules about what students could and could not bring to the dorm. Rules about having cars and using cell phones. Rules about *plagiarism* and *academic integrity*, both of which basically meant no cheating.

There were even rules about what students could wear to class and in the dining hall. Although there was no uniform, the dress code was pretty strict. I could receive a detention just for wearing jeans to the dining hall during the week. Was I going to boarding school or jail?

I had planned to read through the book, sign it, then forget about all the rules, but I didn't even get that far. By page thirty, I was so frustrated that I threw the book across the room.

Maybe the orientation schedule would be more pleasant. It was printed on a sheet of baby blue paper and described my first week of school. I would begin the Thursday after Labor

Day. The schedule listed the times the dining hall would be open for breakfast, lunch, and dinner. There was something called *textbook distribution* each day, although not even my dictionary app could explain what that meant. There were two ceremonies: *matriculation* and *convocation*. Since both words meant the beginning of school, I couldn't understand the difference between the two events.

Most of the schedule, however, was a list of times when everyone would need to register and endless meetings for both new and returning students. But it didn't look like any of them were for me. They were for third, fourth, fifth, and sixth graders.

I frowned at the page. Everything I had read had told me Hartfield was a high school, not an elementary school. I reread the schedule for the first day. After breakfast was registration for students in the third *form*. Wasn't a form a type of letter or paper? How did that relate to grades?

My dictionary app didn't even know. Neither did the internet. Finally, I found an explanation on the Hartfield website.

> Hartfield follows the British tradition of referring to grade levels as *forms*. Our students begin in the third form, corresponding to the American ninth grade, and continue to the sixth form, or twelfth grade.

Great. So all those meetings for third formers were really for me. How was I ever going to get through the upcoming school year? There were so many new rules to follow. So many new people to meet. I would be living in a new place.

And now I was going to need to learn a new language: boarding school.

I threw my vocabulary journal on the floor. Why were my parents doing this to me?

Chapter 6

I SPENT MOST OF MY JULY AND AUGUST WITH CASEY and Brittany. I was determined to make this the best summer ever. Because once school started in the fall, things were going to change.

Not too much, of course. I intended to text and video chat with them every day. Maybe my parents would let me come home on the weekends. I could still see my friends.

But, despite my confidence, every time we went to the movies or had a sleepover, I had a feeling in the pit of my stomach that after I started Hartfield, I would never see Brittany and Casey again. This would be our last summer together.

While I was with my friends, my mother did a lot of shopping for my dorm. By late August, my things were piling up in the living room. My mother had bought me four new sheet sets—two for warm weather and two for winter—as well as a blanket and a fluffy new comforter. She had also bought me a throw blanket and a new pillow.

Somewhere during the middle of the summer, she brought me to the mall to buy new clothes, since a lot of what I owned did not conform to the dress code of my new school. While I thought that should have signaled my parents that they were making a mistake sending me there, they ignored my protests and continued shopping.

My mother had found some dorm packing lists and bought nearly everything on it. I now owned a shower basket for my shampoo and soap, although I couldn't understand why I couldn't leave them in my shower like I did at home. Sure, I would probably have to share a shower with another girl or two, but we could just label our stuff, right?

Although I didn't have a class schedule, my mother took me shopping for my regular back-to-school supplies. Based on what she had discussed with my guidance counselor, as well as the admissions office, she was confident I would have five classes: English, science, math, a foreign language, and an elective. I spent a long time debating whether I should buy one big binder for all my classes or separate smaller ones for each subject, eventually settling on the latter.

Not all my school supplies were new, however. I was bringing my bedside alarm clock and the laptop I had gotten for my birthday. And my dance bag, since I might take some classes at Hartfield.

Unlike my new private school, my brother and my friends started their classes the last week in August. I was very bored waiting for them to come home. I repacked my bags more times than I could count. I spent my days wandering the living room, checking my piles, daydreaming about what my new life might be like.

The night before I was to leave, my mother insisted I go with her to run errands. I didn't want to. I was hoping to call my friends. Maybe text Eliot as we had been doing all summer. But she was insistent.

Begrudgingly, I huffed into the car, brooding all the way to her first stop: Brittany's house. I didn't even want to get out of the car, but my mother insisted I run something inside.

I was halfway through the door when I realized she was following me. Why hadn't she just done it herself?

Brittany's mother smiled at me. "Hey, sweetie. Brittany's doing her homework. I bet she'd love to see you."

Reluctantly, I made my way upstairs. I was so frustrated with my mother, I wasn't even in the mood to see my friend. I was tempted to sneak back to the car.

But I wouldn't see Brittany again for a while, so I continued up the stairs. I couldn't leave without saying goodbye. Maybe when we left, I could convince my mother to bring me to Casey's house as well.

Brittany had shut her door, but that didn't surprise me. She always kept it closed. And I always entered without knocking.

"Surprise!"

I was floored. Standing with Brittany were Casey and a few other girls from school. I had known all of them since the second grade. And they were all here to see me off. I was too overcome to say a word.

Brittany threw her arms around me. "Were you surprised?"

I could only nod.

Casey hugged me next. "We've been planning this *all* week."

Brittany thrusted a wrapped package at me. "We made this for you."

I unwrapped the present carefully, staring at it for a moment. At one point in time, it was probably a shoebox. But it was now covered in magazine clippings. Around pictures of people hugging each other were words relating to friends and friendship. The girls had cut some from the magazines, but they had also handwritten many of them in pen and marker as well.

I removed the lid, slowly sifting through the contents. It was mostly photos of me with my friends. Brittany and Casey, as well as all the other girls in the room. Near the bottom was a coupon for refrigerated pizza dough that made me smile.

One night last spring, Brittany and I tried to make our own pizza, but we had done something wrong. The dough hadn't cooked properly. Instead of returning it to the oven, we ended up eating the entire pizza raw. The event had been so memorable that Brittany had even mentioned it in my yearbook.

Beneath the coupon was a small toy skunk. The memory brought tears to my eyes.

It had been my first playdate at Casey's house. Our mothers sent us outside while they had coffee in the kitchen. Casey's yard ended in a large area full of trees, and I had loved my new friend's suggestion of playing hide and seek in the woods.

I found an area with a few old logs arranged in a fort just the right size for a tiny six-year-old. I crawled inside, waiting for Casey to finish counting. A small cat approached. He was black with a white stripe extending from his head to the tip of his tail. Casey had told me about her new puppy, but she had never mentioned a cat.

I longed to pet it, but I didn't want Casey to find me. Keeping my voice low, I whispered as softly as I could.

"Here, kitty, kitty."

The cat startled and stared at me. I reached out my hand, but the cat skirted backward. It turned and lifted its tail. And peed all over me.

It smelled disgusting. Screaming, I burst into tears. Casey appeared as I was crawling out of my fort.

"Found you! Eww. You smell bad. That's what I'm going to call you. Smelly Melly. That's your new name."

Smiling, I gave Casey an enormous hug. "Thank you so much."

"I'm going to miss you, Smelly Melly!"

At the bottom of the box was a letter written in Casey's beautiful penmanship.

Dear Melinda,
    You have truly been a great friend to all of us over the years. We have shared so many memories together. So many secrets. We will truly miss you. Please don't forget us at your fancy new school. We love you.

Every girl at the party had signed the letter. My heart overflowed with happiness. I couldn't believe my friends had done all this just for me. I felt so loved. The tears that had been brewing since I climbed out of the car finally spilled over. But, my friends didn't make fun of me. Some of them were crying, too.

To help brighten everyone's spirits, Brittany turned on some music and the girls told me about their new high school. It sounded like a lot had changed and I got the impression that while all these girls had come to see me off, they weren't hanging out with each other anymore.

Since it was a school night, the girls weren't allowed to stay long. Parents and older siblings soon collected my friends until I was alone with Brittany and Casey. I pulled both of them into my arms.

"Thank you so much for the party, you guys!"

Casey shook her head mournfully. "High school is so different from middle school, Smelly. And it's just weird that you're not there with us."

Brittany nodded. "I have no one to talk to during English class. I'm so lonely."

My mother interrupted us, calling me from the bottom of the stairs. "Melinda? We have to go!"

I quickly hugged each of my friends one last time and they walked me to the door. I cradled my shoebox close to my chest the entire drive home. My mother tried to ask me about the party, but I didn't want to tell her. Something special had happened that night and I worried that if I shared it with anyone, the magic would disappear.

As soon as I got home, I rushed upstairs to my room. Settling on my bedroom floor, I looked through my box again, not bothering to stop the tears. After reliving each memory one last time, I found a special place on my closet shelf for my shoebox. Even though I was leaving for Hartfield tomorrow, I was confident I had enough memories of my friends to last until I could see them again.

Chapter 7

MOVING DAY HAD FINALLY ARRIVED. AS SOON AS MY brother's school bus pulled away from the curb, I followed my parents into the car that my father had packed while I was at Brittany's. Before we even pulled out of the garage, I shoved headphones in my ear and blasted music louder than my parents. I didn't want to spend the next two hours listening to them remind me why this new school was a good idea.

I was nearly asleep when my father pulled off the highway, but it still took another half an hour before we arrived at my new school. At least, I was pretty sure it was Hartfield. I couldn't be positive because it didn't look like any school I had ever attended.

My father stopped at a four-way intersection, and I tried to find Hartfield. Walking paths extended in all directions from here, leading to houses and buildings of various shapes and sizes. Scattered along the paths were people, a little older than me, wearing bright yellow shirts. On their backs, *MAY I HELP YOU* was written in big block letters.

My father passed through the intersection, and I examined the closest house. There was a little white sign near the front door, though I couldn't read it. The next building held the same sign. Maybe they were both part of Hartfield? But neither looked large enough to hold classes. Or to house nearly one thousand students.

My father pulled into a driveway on the right. In the distance, I saw two large brick buildings. One of these was probably my new school.

I climbed out of the car, glancing around as I stretched. The driveway where we had parked ran between two sports fields. Soccer or football, probably. At the corner where it met the road were some white stakes with large arrows. The one that read *REGISTRATION* pointed across the street.

My parents headed in that direction. With a shrug, I followed them. As we approached, I realized we were walking toward two buildings with floor-to-ceiling glass facing each other, connected by a large concrete staircase. Between them, a modest courtyard held a small red tree and a few random abstract sculptures. Lining the path were flags with tiny labels on the ground beneath them. The ones on my right were different countries, while those on the left represented nearly every state. I got the impression these flags were significant, though I couldn't imagine why they were there.

Another white sign pointed us into the building on the right. There was more concrete here, including a spiral staircase in the middle of the room leading to a loft. A glass office stood to my right while low couches and tables in purples and blues dotted around the room. Artwork and sculptures hung on the walls under the loft.

I frowned. This room gave the impression of a fancy art gallery. Hopefully, this wouldn't be where I was living.

Along the glass wall hung a Hartfield banner. Beneath it were three folding tables, a well-dressed adult behind each. I followed my parents to the one labeled "L-S".

Behind it sat a thin woman with long brown hair wearing a black pantsuit with a pink blouse. As we approached, she stood with a smile.

"Good morning! Welcome to Hartfield! What's your name?"

Although my parents were in front of me, the woman was looking straight at me. I bit my lip. "Uh, Melinda. Melinda Luzzelli."

The woman smiled. "Melinda! It's so nice to meet you. My name is Sally Hunter, but you can call me Sally. I'm one of your house advisors and the third form dean." I had no idea what she meant, but she didn't seem to be waiting for my response. She scanned a paper beside her, marked my name with a highlighter, and rifled through the box in front of her. A moment later, she pulled out a black glossy folder not unlike the one I had received this summer.

Sally opened the folder between us, pointing to the first paper on the left. "This is your class schedule. Bring it with you when you get your textbooks this week, and you'll need it during your orientation meetings tomorrow." She pointed to the page facing it. "This is the schedule for the week. The dining hall will be open for lunch soon, but you have plenty of time if you'd like to move into your dorm first."

Sally pulled a sheet of paper from behind my class schedule. "Here is a map of the campus. As you can see, we're here at the Visual and Performing Arts Center." She indicated a strange shape labeled VAPAC. "Woodward is across the street over here." After pointing to a square near the top of the page, she again opened the folder, gesturing to a key taped to the left pocket. "You're in room 210. That's on the second floor, of course."

Nodding, I accepted the folder and turned to my parents. "Uh, I guess we should go move in?"

I followed them back to the car, and my father drove to the building known as Woodward. My new home. I was a little shocked that it had a name.

Vehicles lined the narrow drive, but my father squeezed between two cars behind a three-story building. The first floor was brick, while the upper ones were a freshly painted white clapboard.

I grabbed my backpack and black folder before making my way up the wide steps. Taking a deep breath, I passed through the open double doors into my new home.

A tiny foyer led to a large living room. Several library study tables dotted the space, scattered between petite couches. Tall windows held small seats and I could easily picture myself curling up to read in one. Maybe I would have some time to do so tonight.

Hallways extended to my right and left. The people moving through them were creating a lot of noise as they carried their belongings to their new homes.

In the center of the living room stood two girls in bright yellow shirts. The shorter one approached me with a smile.

"Hi! I'm Adrienne. I'm the second-floor prefect. What's your name?"

Her enthusiasm was a little over the top. Who was that excited to be moving into school?

I bit my lip. "Uh, Melinda. Melinda Luzzelli."

"Oh! Great! You're on my floor. Let's go find your room!"

Adrienne bounded down the hallway to my right. I followed, my parents closely behind me. She led us up a flight of switchback stairs on my left that dumped us almost directly above where we had started. After turning right, she glanced at the doors on either side of the hall before stopping in front of number 210.

"There you go!" Adrienne gestured to the door.

Someone had taped two large red paper apples to the front. My name was on the one on the right. The one on the left said *Sarah*.

The door was ajar. I pushed it open to find a room a little larger than my bedroom at home. Directly ahead of me, two desks faced the wall on either side of a single window. Through the open curtain, I could see the VAPAC in the distance.

On my right stood a bed elevated so the bare mattress was about level with my hip. At its foot was a matching wardrobe. The furniture on the left mirrored that on the right, except the entire side of the room felt less barren.

Posters of puppies adorned the wall. On the desk sat a laptop and lamp. The bed contained a pink comforter that matched the decorative pillows.

It also held a girl laying on her stomach, feet in the air with her head to the door. She glanced in my direction as I entered, pushing back her long black hair.

She jumped to her feet. "Hi, Roomie! You must be Melinda. I'm Sarah Tran!"

My eyes widened, but I didn't say a word. I couldn't. I was in too much shock. Throughout the summer, I had imagined my life in the dorm. But never once did it occur to me that I might have to share my room with a complete stranger.

I glanced behind me to ask my parents if they had been aware of this roommate thing. But they had disappeared. Great. They had abandoned me. Adrienne was missing, too. I was alone with this strange girl.

I turned back to her. Like me, she was about five-foot-nothing. And she was looking at me expectantly. Had she asked me a question?

I bit my lip. "Sorry. I'm a little overwhelmed with everything."

She smiled. "That's okay. I was, too, when I first went to boarding school. Anyway, I was saying that if you wanted to raise or lower your bed, I could help you."

I shook my head. "Nah. It's . . . it's fine like that, I guess."

Sarah looked around. "I'm all moved in. You want me to help you get your stuff?"

"Uh, sure. Why not?"

As I followed Sarah out of the room, I realized that my parents had probably already returned to the car. Sure enough, they were pulling all my things from the trunk, piling them in the grass beside the car.

I was still wearing my backpack and carrying my folder. In my shock over my new living arrangements, I had forgotten to leave them behind. Sarah and I each grabbed a plastic tub and returned to the room.

Sarah placed the box she was carrying on her own bed and turned to me. "Why don't you put everything on my side of the room for now?"

I glanced around. "You sure?"

"Yeah. It'll make it easier to unpack. You'll see."

With a shrug, I placed the box on her bed and my backpack near her desk. My mother appeared a moment later with the large plastic tub containing my bedding.

"I'm getting too old for those stairs. Did anyone find the elevator?"

Sarah shook her head. "This dorm doesn't have one."

My mother frowned. "Well, tell you what. Why don't you girls go get the rest of the boxes while I stay here and make the bed?"

I shrugged. "Yeah, I guess."

Four grueling trips later, the car was empty. But the room was full. With all my boxes, plus all of us, I felt claustrophobic.

Sarah turned to my parents. "Mr. and Mrs. Luzzelli? Why don't you go get lunch? The dining hall should be open soon. I'll help Melinda unpack and we can meet you there."

My mother turned to me. "Melinda?"

I gave a small nod. "Yeah. That's not a bad idea."

"Do you know the way? I would hate for you to get lost."

Sarah smiled. "I was here over the summer. Melinda will be fine."

As I waved goodbye to my parents, I was pretty sure this was the part of the horror movie where my roommate was going to kill me. I eyed her suspiciously as she closed the door.

Hands on hips, she turned to me. But her face didn't scream murder. It was screwed up in confusion.

"Okay. Where should we start? Your mom made your bed and hung your clothes. What if you load the rest of your clothes into the drawers and I can unpack your desk supplies?"

I shrugged. "Yeah, that works, but . . ."

It was incredibly nice of her to offer to help me, but how could I explain that I didn't want her touching my belongings? I had to know where everything was so I could find things when I needed them.

Sarah seemed to understand. She smiled. "Don't worry. I'm just going to stack everything on top. You get to put it away."

As I folded my underwear into one of the wardrobe drawers, I glanced at my new roommate. "You're pretty good at this moving in thing."

Sarah pulled my desk lamp from the box with a shrug. "I've been in boarding school since the fourth grade. And usually at least one summer program each year. I've lost track of how many times I've moved into and out of the dorms."

I wasn't sure what to say. How could her parents be so cruel that Sarah spent more time in boarding school than with them? But she didn't seem to be bitter about the situation like I would have been. I opted against saying anything.

When I finished with my clothes, I shoved my dance bag into the space between the wardrobe and door that seemed to have been made for it. Sarah and I then switched places. While she unpacked my toiletries onto the bed, I sorted my desk supplies.

After finding homes for all the little things, I set my laptop in the middle of the desk, plugging it in to charge. I placed my lamp and alarm clock on the right, within arms-reach of my bed beside it. Hopefully, those little comforts would help make this place feel more like home.

Chapter 8

ABOUT HALF AN HOUR LATER, MY SIDE OF THE ROOM no longer looked neglected.

Sarah threw an arm around my shoulders. "Okay, Roomie. I say that deserves a lunch break. What do you think?"

Nodding, I grabbed my key from the black folder and slipped it into my jeans pocket before following my roommate out of the dorm. My parents' car was no longer in the driveway. Other families were unloading their cars.

Sarah seemed to know her way around already. She turned right out of the dorm and headed toward the main road. Along the way, we passed a large building similar to our dorm. Except, it was as if someone had raised it in the air and stuck one more floor underneath the first level. It wasn't just that it was taller. The main entrance appeared to be on the second floor, at the top of a very wide concrete staircase.

I pointed to it as we passed. "What's that building?"

Sarah followed my gaze. "Oh. That's Stanton. I'm pretty sure it's a boys' dorm. And that's Humanities."

I had no idea what Sarah meant by *humanities*, but I was too embarrassed to ask. Instead, I stared at where she was pointing, the last building along our path instead. It looked similar to the two dorms. Brick first level and white trim, although a large semicircle was sticking out of the middle.

After crossing the street, Sarah led me to two more brick buildings that seemed to be joined by a covered walkway. She pointed to the first one. "That's the library."

Like the boys' dorm, the second building had a large concrete staircase, nearly as wide as the front, leading to the second story entrance. However, Sarah detoured to a smaller set of stairs up to the covered walkway and led me through a side door instead.

We passed a row of offices, emerging into another living room with three low couches arranged around a fireplace. Above the mantle hung a painting of the school's founder, according to the tiny brass plate at the bottom of the frame.

The room had a very antique feeling. I bit my lip as we passed through. "Uh, Sarah? Are we supposed to be in here?"

She giggled. "Yeah, it's fine. I lived in the dorm upstairs over the summer. This was one of my favorite common rooms. I hope they light the fire in the winter."

I wasn't convinced, but I said nothing. Instead, I followed Sarah around the fireplace to another hallway. She pointed to a staircase tucked into the right.

"That's where I lived this summer. But I think it's a boys' dorm during the year."

We passed through a set of double doors and I stopped dead in my tracks. I had assumed the dining hall would be like the cafeterias in my elementary or middle school. But this was no cafeteria.

The ceilings had to be at least ten feet tall, maybe higher. It made the room feel massive. In front of me was an enormous fireplace with a mantle of dark oak. Stone surrounded it, working its way upward to form a chimney nearly as wide as the hearth.

The room was lined in with the same dark wood as the mantle, with tall windows deep set to create ledges large enough to be seats. On the walls between them were giant plaques listing recipients of various school awards over the past century and a half.

On either side of the room were four round wooden tables with eight matching chairs around each. They looked like something I would find in my grandmother's dining room, not what I would have envisioned for my school's cafeteria.

As I followed my roommate toward the fireplace, I frowned. How were all the students in the school expected to eat at only eight tables? And where was the food?

My questions were quickly answered without me having to voice them aloud. As soon as I stepped around the hearth, I saw the rest of the dining hall.

It surprised me to see the fireplace also opened on this side, a section with several salad bars, including a made-to-order sandwich station under the windows to my right. Directly in front of me was an area about the size of my middle school cafeteria, filled with many more of the dining tables I had seen when I first entered.

To the left of it was a half-wall about the size of my waist, with pillars every few feet that extended to the ceiling. There were even more tables on the other side of the half-wall. People were entering this special room through two wide-arched entrances, one on either side of the half-wall.

I didn't realize I was staring until Sarah appeared in front of me. "Lemme show you where to get your tray."

She led me to a small room on my left. I instantly recognized it as the servery, since it looked at least a little like the one in my middle school. She gestured to the right of the entrance.

"There you go. I usually just grab a tray and then come back for my silverware."

That was good advice, since I had no idea what I was having for lunch. I followed my roommate to a small cart, grabbing a blue plastic tray from the dispenser. At the top, I noticed cups separating the silverware. Real metal forks, knives, and spoons, not the plastic sporks they had at my old school.

I lost Sarah as soon as I passed through the doors. The servery was about the size of the one at my middle school, although it felt much cleaner. In the center of the room was a beverage island with crates of drinking glasses nestled between a multitude of dispensers. In addition to soda and juice fountains, I saw unusual metal cylinders that looked like small silos. I watched a woman place a glass beneath it and lift the strange handle. A white substance that could only be milk flowed into the cup.

Shaking my head, I surveyed my options. Along the three sides of the room were cafeteria counters divided into several stations. Behind one, a server was laying out pizzas. Beside it was a self-service pasta bar. A cereal bar was tucked into the corner to my left, with clear dispensers filled with the sugary cereals my brother liked as well as the healthier ones I preferred.

On the opposite side of the room, a server was scooping the hot entrée of the day onto a plate. It looked like something with fries, but I couldn't be sure. At a large griddle in the back of the room, a server was making a grilled sandwich, the cheese oozing between the two slices of bread.

Tucked into the corner on my right was the dessert station, a small display case of cookies beside another with slices of cakes and pies.

The food looked delicious, but I was so overwhelmed, I had lost my appetite. With a sigh, I returned to the salad bar. The first one held two vats of soup, along with containers of peanut butter, several jellies, something I assumed to be hummus, and more types of bread than I ever thought possible. The second bar contained lettuce and toppings too numerous to count.

But it still wasn't what I wanted. I needed comfort food. And while a grilled cheese sounded good, a sandwich might be better.

The woman behind the counter smiled as I approached. "Good afternoon. What can I get for you?"

"Uh, I'll have a turkey sandwich, I guess."

Nodding, the server reached for a ceramic plate beside her. "What kind of bread would you like?"

"What kind of bread?"

I was so used to my mother making my food, I had never really considered what went into creating a sandwich. I glanced at the selection beside her. "Um, white, I guess."

"And what kind of cheese?"

"Um, American?"

I watched the server arrange the bread on the plate, place a slice of cheese on each, then fold three pieces of turkey onto one side before passing the plate to me. Thanking her, I brought my tray to the salad bar, where I added mayonnaise and lettuce to the sandwich.

With a sigh, I looked around. I needed to find my roommate. And my parents. And the dining hall was growing crowded. How would I find anyone? Maybe the mass of people would engulf me and I could forget that this humongous place was supposed to be my new home.

"All set?"

Turning to the voice, I found Sarah standing beside me. I shrugged. "I guess."

Sarah pointed to my tray. "Did you want a drink?"

I sighed. "A drink would be nice."

I carried my tray into the servery, resting it on the rails while I grabbed a glass. Even this machine had too many choices. But diet cola was always my favorite. Besides, maybe the caffeine would make me feel less overwhelmed.

As I stepped out of the servery, I caught sight of the salad bar. And a man near the dressings. Could it be? Was my imagination playing tricks on me, or was my father really right there?

The man turned. It *was* my father! I wanted to run and hug him. I was so excited to see a familiar face in this sea of strangers that, for a moment, I forgot I was still mad he was sending me to this foreign place.

But I didn't run. I took a few steps closer and waited for him to notice me.

After building his salad, he looked up, smiling at me and waving with his free hand.

"We were wondering when we'd see you girls." He nodded toward the smaller dining section. "We've got a table over here."

Sarah and I followed my father to the table, where my mother was reading through the black folder I had received when we registered. She smiled as we sat across from her.

"Are you all moved in?"

Moved in implied this was my new home and I was comfortable here. And it wasn't. But I had found a place for all my belongings. I shrugged. "I think so."

Sarah shook her head. "I don't know about you, but I still need to buy my textbooks."

I was beyond confused. I had never had to purchase school books before. I frowned. "Don't the teachers just hand them out in class?"

My mother shook her head. "No, Melinda. Hartfield is like college. You need to buy your books at the school store. But they're yours to keep. You don't have to return them at the end of the year, so you can mark them however you want."

My mind flashed back to the girl I had seen at the coffee shop the day after learning about Hartfield. She had been highlighting her textbook. Is that what my mother meant? Why would I ever want to make marks in a book?

Sarah grabbed the pastel yellow paper sitting in the center of the table. I glanced at it over her shoulder. It was the *Daily Docket*, just like the one I had been reading online. Today, it looked nearly identical to the orientation schedule in my mother's folder.

Sarah glanced at her phone, probably to check the time. "Hey. We have a couple of hours till our first meeting. We should go get our books now, before the line gets too long."

My mother smiled. "That's an excellent idea. I was talking to a woman near the salad bar and she said it took her over an hour to get her son's books. May I see that?"

Sarah passed her the paper as I stared at my sandwich. I was losing my appetite again.

My mother nodded as she reviewed the page. "Yes. I think we will have just enough time to get books before the first meeting. We won't really have time after. Is that okay with you, Melinda?"

I shrugged. Did I really have a choice? Besides, what else was I going to do? Sit in Room 210 and sulk and hide and never come out because the mere size of this new school was overwhelming and scaring me?

Sarah turned to me. "I need to go back to my room to get my schedule before I go to the MAC."

What was the MAC? My mother didn't give me a chance to ask. She frowned at the map in her hand. "Why don't we go get in line? You can grab your schedule and meet us there."

Sarah nodded. "That's a great idea. Can we go right now? Is everyone done?"

Since our plates were empty, I thought it was obvious. But Sarah waited for my parents to nod before getting to her feet. We mirrored her actions, placing our empty plates and glasses onto our trays.

In my middle school, we had deposited our trash in the large barrels that stood near the exit. I didn't see any in this dining hall. Not that I expected to throw away ceramic dishes and real flatware and glasses. I glanced around. No one had left dirty trays on their tables, either. So what were we supposed to do with these things?

Sarah was taking hers back to the servery. My parents and I grabbed our things and followed her, turning into a small room beside the servery. She placed her tray on a conveyor belt before removing her flatware and napkin. I watched her sort these into labeled holes in front of the belt as her tray disappeared through a door to some unknown region of the dining hall.

After my parents and I disposed of our trays similarly, Sarah brought us back to the servery entrance. Pointing at the map in my mother's hands, she gave my parents some directions before heading out a door near the sandwich bar. I followed my parents out the way I had entered.

Chapter 9

MY PARENTS EXITED THE BUILDING USING A DOOR near the common room, and I found myself at the top of the concrete staircase I had seen from afar. I took a moment to glance around. To my right was yet another building with a brick bottom and white trim. Were they all built at the same time? Or did the school just want everything to match?

A driveway circled in front of the buildings in this area and I saw a few Victorian-style houses that seemed to have escaped the brick trend. One was a powder blue while the other was a cheerful cream.

My parents were already at the bottom of the stairs. I hurried to catch up with them. My mother pointed to a smaller building—again, brick and white—as we passed. "That's the chapel. I remember seeing that on our campus tour."

While she consulted her map, I silently followed my parents along the walkway until it ended at the main road. The cars in both directions stopped, allowing us to cross. The path continued on the other side, passing more houses and larger buildings, most of which did not match the brick and white trend. Since people were moving boxes into the main doors, I assumed they were dormitories.

When we had first arrived at Hartfield that morning, I had seen a brick building I had assumed was my new school. This was where my parents were now heading. I glanced around. From where I stood, I could see the VAPAC where we had registered. I could almost see my dorm and the dining hall. If I considered these four buildings to be a square, maybe I would someday be able to find my way around as well as my roommate.

I turned my attention back to the brick and white cube we were approaching. The front steps were nearly as wide as the building, but there were only four, not an entire story like the dining hall. A plaque beside the door named this place the *MacMillan Activities Center*, and I instantly understood why Sarah had called it the *MAC*.

The double doors opened into a small foyer with stairs going up and down. Passing through another set of double doors, my parents and I walked into a madhouse. There were people everywhere.

A glass office was directly in front of us, and through it I could see a long line of people. Why? What could possibly be such a big deal? I turned slowly to my right, trying to find the front of the line. Through the glass, I could see more of those little common room couches arranged around a television hanging from the ceiling.

I kept turning. The line ended in front of another little area with couches and televisions. People were on either side of a folding table. I watched as a boy lifted a pile of books from it and make his way toward the exit behind me. *Seriously?* All these people were here to buy books?

Sighing, I tried to find the end of the line. As I turned, I glanced beyond the waiting people. The stage was only a couple of steps above the ground, but it formed most of the back half of the room. Folding tables were in long rows. I couldn't see how many because of all the heads in my way, but it looked to be a lot. Stacks of books covered the tables. Big stacks and small stacks. Thick books and thin books.

A man was wandering through the rows, consulting the page in his hand before grabbing three books from the table. After scanning each with a handheld device, he placed them in the basket dangling on his arm and wandered to another table.

"Do you need help finding something?"

I turned to the girl who had asked. She was wearing one of those yellow shirts. Biting my lip, I glanced around. Where were my parents? I wanted to say, "I'm all alone. Have you seen my Mommy and Daddy?" But I didn't think that was appropriate in high school.

I turned back to the girl beside me. "I think my parents got themselves lost?"

She smiled. "I'm going to suggest the book line. That's where most people start. You want me to help you find them?"

What was I, five? Did I look that pathetic? I shook my head. "No, but thanks."

"No problem."

I turned to the left, intending to find my parents. The scene reminded me of the sales area at my father's annual accounting conventions. Card tables lined the room, each with a bored salesperson behind it. I recognized the names of several local banks. I saw a few cell phone companies. Beside another was a pile of lavender bags that looked large enough for me to fit inside. People blocked my view of the other tables. People like my parents.

With a sigh of relief, I headed toward them, still looking at the sales area. Behind the vendors were some arcade games and pool tables. Although they were shut down for the day, I could see myself maybe enjoying spending time here when they were open.

My parents were at the back of the line. I no sooner joined them when Sarah appeared beside me.

"Hey, Roomie. Wow! There are a lot of people here."

My mother nodded. "Yeah, but I think it will go pretty quickly. We've only been here a couple of minutes and we've already moved a few feet."

I pointed to the sales tables. "Any idea what all that is?"

Sarah shook her head. "No. Let's go check it out when we're done with our books."

My mother bit her lip. "I'm worried we won't have time."

My father stepped to the side to peer at the front of the line before turning back to us. "Tell you what. Why don't the three of you go take a look? I'll save our places. If I get near the front, I'll text you."

My mother nodded. "Perfect."

The first table Sarah wanted to visit was the woman with the lavender sacks. She smiled as we approached.

"Good afternoon. Are you interested in enrolling in Hartfield's laundry service?"

My mother frowned. "Can you explain how this works?"

She could. In a lot of detail. It took her longer than it should have to explain that I should put my dirty laundry in the bag, leave it outside my door on Wednesday mornings, and someone would wash, fold, and return it to me by the end of the day. When the woman finally stopped babbling, my mother turned to me.

"What do you think, Melinda? Would you like to sign up? Or would you rather do your own laundry?"

Sarah grimaced. "I did my laundry over the summer. It's kind of far to carry all your dirty clothes every week."

That was enough to convince me. I turned to my mother. "Can I have the service?"

After Sarah and I had both enrolled, the woman rewarded us each with a lavender bag. We browsed through the other tables, but no one else was selling anything that we wanted to buy. Sarah and I both had cell phones and debit cards at our parents' banks. After touring the room, we returned to the book line. My father was closer to the table, but there were still many people in front of him. Sarah turned to my mother.

"Mrs. Luzzelli? Can I show Melinda the loft super quick?"

My mother nodded. "Of course."

Our line had passed a tall staircase. I followed Sarah to the top, where a large room separated the loft into two parts.

I pointed to the bright red lockers on the right. "Any idea what those are for?"

Sarah frowned. "If I had to guess, day students?"

"Who?"

Sarah giggled. "People who live close enough to commute instead of living in the dorms."

I could have done that? Sure, maybe not Hartfield, but couldn't my parents find a school closer to us?

Shaking my head, I followed Sarah to the other side of the loft. She pointed to the room in the center.

"That's the snack bar. Over the summer, it was open from the end of the class day until study hours."

I glanced at the menu above the closed service window. It was mostly grilled meals and snacks, including some of my favorites. I turned back to Sarah. "Is the food any good?"

"It's not bad. Hey. Come check this out."

She leaned over the nearest railing and I followed suit. Below us, people were scanning books and placing them into baskets. It was almost mesmerizing, but we couldn't stay. Sarah needed to be in line to get her books.

My roommate led me to the other set of stairs in the front of the building, which brought us back to the main entrance. The book line was almost at the doors now and I was glad we had come when we had. We walked beside the waiting people until we found my parents. Perfect timing. They were next in line.

A man passed the girl in front of us an overflowing basket and turned to my mother. "Schedule?"

Nodding, she passed the sheet to the man.

"New or used?"

I had no idea what he meant, but my mother must have. "New, please."

A woman was beside Sarah a moment later. My roommate didn't wait to be asked before holding out her schedule. "Used, please."

The woman nodded. "Of course."

A few minutes later, the man returned with my basket. It was overflowing. He placed it beside one of the people standing behind the folding table at the end of the line. While my mother swiped her card in the reader, the person transferred all the books into a large paper shopping bag with handles. Sarah was paying by the time the person passed me my bag.

I nearly dropped it. Was I really expected to carry all these books *every day*? How would they even fit into my backpack?

When we left the building, Sarah led us along a path that went directly to the four-way intersection. There were too many cars for us to cross diagonally, but someone waved us through on one of the streets. As we waited for a driver to let us cross the other road, I could see my dorm. Maybe by the end of the day, I would be able to get there on my own.

Chapter 10

SARAH AND I HAD JUST ENOUGH TIME TO EMPTY OUR books onto our desks before our first meeting of the day. Armed with our black folders, Sarah led the way to the VAPAC. Remembering my square map, it didn't surprise me to see her turn left out of our dorm, leading me and my parents down the driveway to a path I had yet to travel. After crossing the street, we went around other buildings to arrive at the side of the VAPAC.

People were streaming into the area from all directions. Some were chatting excitedly. Others looked as afraid as I felt. Instead of entering the side where we had registered, they were using the other entrance. People in yellow shirts showed us how to enter the theater.

Unlike many auditoriums, the doors did not bring us to the back of the room. Instead, I found myself standing on the side of a long row of seats. Although there was a balcony, no one was directing us to it. Students and their parents were all crammed into the orchestra level.

76

My father pointed down a row and started climbing over everyone sitting to reach seats only he seemed able to see, my mother in his wake. By the time I followed, most of the people in our way had either stood to let us pass or pulled their feet onto the chairs.

Our timing was perfect. We were still settling into our seats when a man stepped out of the wings, stopping at a podium near the center of the stage. He was a little taller than my father and on the stocky side. His powder blue shirt complemented his navy suit. Pushing his wire-rimmed glasses up his nose, he tapped the microphone with his other hand. The room fell silent.

"Good afternoon. For those of you whom I have not yet met, my name is Mr. Birkenhead and I am the third form boys' dean."

I leaned closer to my mother, keeping my voice low. "What's a dean?"

She frowned. "Like the principal, but just for your grade. Now, shh. This is important."

Nodding, I turned my attention back to the stage. Sally had just introduced herself. The two of them then went into a long speech about the history of the school before summarizing the rest of our meetings for the night.

I stopped paying attention. None of this was new information. I had read most of the history in the school handbook and the rest online. The schedule was in the folders we were all holding. So far, I had been at Hartfield for three hours and was as bored as I had been last year. I should have stayed in public school.

Out of the corner of my eye, I saw Sarah rise to her feet. I looked around. Other students were standing, climbing over adults to get to the end of the rows. I followed Sarah out of the theater.

While a few people in yellow shirts were leading students up the concrete stairs, almost everyone else was walking back to the dormitory. I tried not to roll my eyes as I followed my roommate. We were *just there*. Why had we even bothered with the theater?

Since no one else was complaining, I held my tongue and followed my new classmates across the field to Woodward. Every girl in our dorm was crowded into the common room. Six squeezed onto couches that were only meant for about three or four people. Each window seat held at least two girls, sometimes three. My new classmates were sitting on coffee tables and end tables and study tables. Sarah and I squeezed onto the floor beside each other between a couch and study table.

Even though the room was packed, it was almost silent. Probably because we were all strangers. We were all staring at the four girls in the center of the room wearing their bright yellow shirts.

One of them glanced around. "I think that's everyone. Well, for anyone I didn't meet earlier, my name is Melissa. I'm the prefect on the garden floor, which is just a fancy name for the basement."

There were a few polite giggles as the rest of the girls introduced themselves. Kate was the prefect on the first floor, Adrienne the second, and Bethany the third. Bethany then gestured around the room.

"You are all going to have a lot of opportunities to get to know each other later, but it's important to know who your neighbors are. Obviously, you're all third formers, but let's just go around the room really quick and tell us your first names and where you're from."

There was no way I was going to remember everyone's names, but I listened politely. I was astonished to hear all the hometowns. I had assumed most students would be from Connecticut while the rest might be from New York, Massachusetts, and Rhode Island. But, my new classmates were from all over the country.

The world, I realized, as students named hometowns from Hong Kong, France, and New Zealand. By the time we had finished our introductions, most of the fifty states had been names, as well as countries from every habitable continent.

Bethany smiled at all of us. "Fantastic. I can't wait to get to know all of you over the next few weeks. We'll have a dorm meeting later tonight to go over all the rules. Right now, we're supposed to be learning the school song."

While the other prefects handed each of us a sheet of paper, Bethany continued. "We sing this song at every school meeting and at football games and just a lot of places. It's really important to learn it. We're going to sing it for you once, then we'll practice together, okay?"

Bethany didn't wait for an answer. She nodded to Kate, who pressed a button on her phone. A song rang out through a tiny Bluetooth speaker in the center of the room.

I followed along as the older girls sang. I did my best to join the second run-through. When Adrienne finally dismissed us, I felt as if I had sung the song a thousand times. I could probably sing it in my sleep. Part of me worried I *would* dream about it that night.

We had some time before dinner, so everyone made a beeline to the stairwells. As soon as I entered my room, I collapsed on my bed. Even though I had done little today, I was exhausted.

Sarah was rifling through her closet, pulling out skirts and dresses, holding them in front of herself in the mirror, and returning them to their hanging home. Propping myself on an elbow, I sent her a curious look.

"What are you doing?"

She didn't look at me. "Trying to find something special dress for dinner."

"What's so special about your dress?" I was comfortable in my jeans and T-shirt. Although I didn't mind wearing the occasional dress, I had never considered one *special*.

Sarah stopped her search long enough to send me a curious look. "You know about the different dress codes, right?"

I shrugged. "No jeans at dinner. No unisex shirts in class."

Sarah nodded. "That's the regular dress code. Tonight's dinner is special dress. We have to wear a dress or, like, a pantsuit or something. Boys are wearing jackets and ties."

"Seriously?" Closing my eyes, I collapsed onto my pillow with a sigh. Would I ever learn everything about boarding school? The longer the day drew on, the more I felt I didn't know. And I still had another day of orientation to suffer through before we even started classes. How many more rules would I learn by then?

Sarah tucked a purple blouse under her chin, staring at herself in the mirror on the inside of the wardrobe door. Holding a skirt in each hand, she flashed one, then the other, in front of her waist, her face screwed in consternation.

I had never put so much effort into choosing an outfit. My standards were simple: clean and relatively unwrinkled. Except for major holidays, like Christmas and Easter, when I only planned ahead to stop my mother from badgering me.

Sarah was still frowning at her reflection when someone knocked on the door.

"Come in!" Without looking up, Sarah tossed one skirt onto the bed, used the free hand to place the shirt on top of it, and returned the other skirt to the closet.

All in the time it took for my parents to open the door. My mother sent me a concerned look.

"We need to get going, Baby Girl."

That was it. No comment on my attempts to decorate my room. No asking about our dorm meeting. No telling me what the parents had learned when they stayed behind.

And, of course, no last-minute change of heart. My mother glanced at her watch. "It's getting late and we need to pick up your brother from his friend's house."

It was official. They were abandoning me. Until this moment, there was a part of me deep down that had been hoping my parents would change their mind at the last minute. That they would realize they made a mistake, pack me and my belongings into the car, and bring me home with them. I had been clinging to that shred of hope since the day they had first mentioned Hartfield.

But they were leaving. I was numb as I hugged my parents for the last time. I wasn't sure when I would see them again.

With small waves in my roommate's direction, my parents left. As my father closed the door behind them, I curled into a ball on my bed. I was crushed, too upset for tears. I grabbed my life-sized stuffed puppy, Bonnie, and turned to the wall.

When I was nine, I had my first sleepover at Brittany's house. At home, I slept with at least five dolls and stuffed animals, but I hadn't packed any because I didn't think it was appropriate at a sleepover party for big girls. When I went to unroll my sleeping bag, however, Bonnie was staring at me. My mother had rolled her into it when I wasn't looking.

Overwhelmed with embarrassment, I tried to hide the dog. But Casey had seen. She grabbed Bonnie with a squeal. All the girls at the party loved my dog and took turns cuddling her until we fell asleep. Bonnie was my sleepover companion for many years.

Although Bonnie had outgrown sleepovers, when I was packing for Hartfield, I couldn't imagine being in a new place without her. Now that my parents had abandoned me, Bonnie was my only friend in this strange new world.

I felt the bed move as someone sat beside me. A moment later, there was a hand on my shoulder. Sarah didn't try to hug me or tell me everything would be alright. Yet, her presence was still as comforting as if Brittany or Casey had been here with me.

Was it possible I had made a new friend?

Eventually, I rolled onto my back, sending Sarah a weak smile. It scared her away. She jumped off my bed and I sighed. So much for making friends.

But Sarah didn't return to her side of the room. She opened my wardrobe and flipped through the limited selection of skirts and dresses. A moment later, she tossed a sundress over me like a blanket.

As we both burst into giggles, I realized I hadn't just made a new friend. Sarah could make me laugh when I wanted to cry. I had found another best friend.

Chapter 11

AS SARAH AND I CHANGED FOR DINNER, I REALIZED there was something about tonight's meal that wasn't making sense to me. I turned to my roommate with a frown.

"So, I thought dinner was like lunch. The dining hall was open during certain times."

Sarah brushed her hair with a nod. "It is."

"Then why do we have to be in front of Hartfield Hall at 5:30?"

Sarah pointed at me with her hairbrush. "You know? That's a good point. Wanna go find out?"

With a nod, I followed Sarah out of the room, joining the stream of girls heading toward the closest stairwell. We met even more in the common room, bottlenecking at the front door.

Outside, the stream of Woodward girls joined the boys exiting Stanton to form a river of third formers crossing the street to the front of the dining hall. Although I was nervous about meeting so many new people all at once, I seemed to be among the few who were hesitant. Around me, everyone was chatting excitedly. Introducing themselves to each other.

Sharing stories about their summers. Comparing Hartfield to their previous schools.

Several adults were waiting for us at the bottom of the dining hall steps. I recognized the deans among them. Sally smiled as we approached.

"Welcome. Please stand along the steps. Don't worry. You'll all fit."

I followed the mass of people, eventually finding myself squeezed between Sarah and another girl about halfway up the steps. After a few minutes, Sally raised her hand. Our crowd fell silent.

"Welcome again. For those of you I haven't met, I am Sally Hunter, dean for the third form girls." As she introduced the rest of the adults, I realized we were standing before the most important people in the school: the deans for all four forms. Sally then pointed to the man on her other side. "And, of course, this is Mr. and Mrs. Philip Weinheimer."

That name sounded familiar. I had read it somewhere, but where? I leaned closer to Sarah, my whisper barely audible. "Who're they?"

"The headmaster and his wife."

I gave a knowing nod. Of course. He had signed a lot of the papers I had read this summer. But, I had missed something important. Mr. Birkenhead was speaking.

"This afternoon, you all learned the school song. Tonight, you will sing for your supper."

A murmur went through the crowd. I heard several people voicing my concerns. Had I learned the song well enough? Were we really having a test on our first day of school? We hadn't even had any classes yet.

And how were they going to test us? There had to be a couple hundred of us standing on the stairs. Would we have to perform individually? That could take hours. And what if I got stage fright and couldn't sing in front of everyone? Would I starve tonight?

Mr. Birkenhead raised his hand for silence. "On the count of three, everyone please sing." He nodded to one of the other deans, who held a small portable speaker over her head. "Ready? One . . . two . . ."

He pressed a button on his phone, and I heard the opening bars to the school song. I was so tired of this music, and so scared of failing, that I barely sang above a whisper. Many of my classmates did the same. It was so lackluster, I could not understand how this had become the school's fight song.

When the music ended, the adults raised their eyebrows at each other before Sally turned to us. "I think you can do much better. I want you to take all your hunger and fatigue and put all your energy into this song. Show me you're hungry!"

Mr. Birkenhead again pressed something on his phone. This time, when the music played, I channeled all my fear and anxiety into the song. I was practically screaming. So were my classmates. I almost enjoyed myself, even if this *was* one of the lamest songs I had ever heard.

Again the music ended and again the adults exchanged glances. My classmates and I waited in silence. As one, the deans turned to face us, grinning as they applauded. I breathed a sigh of relief. I had passed my first test at boarding school. It hadn't been all that difficult. Maybe my classes would be this easy?

Sally again raised her hand for silence. "When you enter the dining hall, you will see your names posted at the entrance.

Beside your name is your table number for this evening. After getting your meal, please proceed to your assigned table, where at least one faculty member will join you. Now, if you would all turn around, you may enter the building in an orderly fashion."

As I pivoted, the people below me tried to climb the steps, crushing me into someone else's rear end. However, they must have realized their efforts were fruitless, because they stepped back and waited for the rest of us to move.

Eventually, Sarah and I made our way into the building, following the tide heading to the dining hall. As soon as we stepped inside, we saw people crowded around several easels. Students were running their fingers along the lists.

I had to check three boards before finding my name. I would be sitting at Table 11. Sarah was at Table 29.

I wanted to cry. I had exactly one friend at this new school and I wasn't even allowed to have dinner with her? Was it too late to call my parents for a ride home?

Sarah grabbed my hand, leading me away from the lists toward the fireplace. The servery doors were closed and the salad bars had disappeared. In their place were two long buffet tables. People queued on both sides of each as the first students scooped food onto their plates.

I didn't have to wait long before reaching the stack of plates at the head of the table. I glanced into the first buffet tray. Something that might have been chicken was swimming in a tan gravy with what I thought were mushrooms. I took a small step backward. The label in front of the tray called the dish *Chicken Marsala.* I wasn't a huge fan of mushrooms, but I liked chicken. I took a small piece.

The beef dish in the next tray also seemed to contain mushrooms, but I had already selected chicken, so I skipped it. At the next tray, I scooped some red potatoes in a buttery garlic sauce onto my plate, making sure not to let them fall into the gravy from my chicken. Even at thirteen, I still hated when my food touched.

After placing a scoop of green bean almandine onto my plate, I grabbed a small wheat roll. I wanted some of the salad in the large bowl at the end of the table, but I had run out of space on my plate. Hoping I could go back for more later, I turned to the dining room.

Everyone was sitting in the main section. I had already lost Sarah in the crowd. With a sigh, I searched for Table 11.

It was directly in front of me. And it was empty. I chose a chair close to Table 1, my back to the smaller eating area, but where I could still see the food. This seat meant I could monitor the buffet line without constantly turning around. When it died down, I could get more food.

Another buffet table had replaced the sandwich bar. It held several drink dispensers. Although a small crowd was forming around them, I was thirsty. Leaving my plate at my seat, I ventured to the beverage bar, reading the labels in front of the jugs. Water. Lemonade. Iced tea. Insulated dispensers at the end had coffee and hot water, with packets of tea and sugar beside it.

After filling a glass with water, I returned to the table to find a boy hovering, probably trying to figure out where to sit. I had no idea what to say to him, so I ignored him, returning directly to my chair and staring at my plate as if it were the most interesting thing in the world.

The boy opted for a seat on my right, leaving an empty chair between us. A few minutes later, a girl sat on my other side, also a seat away. Two more boys sat directly beside her and another girl sat to the right of the first boy.

As the line died down, a tall man approached the table and looked around. He had a bright smile as he sat in the empty seat to my right.

"Welcome, new students. How are we this fine evening?"

We shrugged and there were some murmurings, but I didn't hear any actual responses. Personally, I was too mesmerized by the man's tie to respond. The navy background matched his blazer. Tiny handprints in an assortment of bright colors spattered across it. It was adorable.

He must have seen me staring at it. With a smile, he pointed to it and turned to me. "My daughters gave me this tie."

After we all smiled politely, he continued. "Anyway, I don't think we've been properly introduced. I'm Mr. Henderson, and I live in Katzmann house with my wife and our two little girls. In addition to teaching Latin, I am also head of the language department." He turned to the boy on his right. "How about you? Would you like to tell us a little about yourself?"

The boy shrugged. "I'm Michael. I'm from Boston."

"And you're living in Stanton, I presume?"

The boy sent Mr. Henderson an incredulous look. "Duh!"

Personally, I thought the boy was being a little rude, but our teacher didn't seem to mind. He turned to the girl beside Michael.

She took a sip of her lemonade before responding. "I'm Alexia, but everyone calls me Lexi. I'm from Canterbury, New

Jersey. It's near Trenton. I'm in Woodward. It's been a crazy day, hasn't it? I didn't get to move in until after that meeting where we learned the school song. I had a piano competition in Philly last night. It was arduous, but amazing. My friend and I received a bronze award for our duet. And I won gold for two of my songs and silver for a third. But the competition was interminable, and I accidentally overslept this morning."

Lexi kept talking, but I had no idea what she was saying. Her use of big words gave me the impression she was pretending to be smarter than she really was. Hopefully, she was just nervous and would talk like a normal person when she relaxed a little. Because, by the time she turned to the boy beside her, I felt like she was speaking a foreign language.

Jackson was nearly as tall as Mr. Henderson, and his deep voice held just a hint of the South. "I'm from Alabama and I'm looking forward to trying out for football next week. My local high school promised me a spot on varsity, but I wasn't about to turn down Hartfield just for football."

Michael pointed at him with his fork. "Hopefully, you'll make the team here."

Mr. Henderson nodded. "Well, I'm sure Coach Farnsworth appreciates your sacrifice."

I didn't understand the joke, but smiled politely as Mr. Henderson nodded to the next boy at the table. He was even taller than Jackson, with blonde hair nearly as long as mine pulled into a ponytail at the base of his neck.

He put down his fork to smile at the rest of us. "I'm Noah. I'm from California. The math department recruited me for the math team."

Michael interrupted, bits of potato flying out of his mouth as he spoke. "The math team? That's a thing?"

Noah shrugged. "Yeah. I'm taking calculus this term, so Mr. Davidson was pretty sure I would be on the varsity team. But I wouldn't mind JV for a year."

I kind of agreed with Noah. Math team almost sounded fun. Although, I would never admit it aloud. Then again, at a school like Hartfield, it was a little surprising that there wasn't a waiting list to join the team.

The girl between me and Noah looked a little older than me. She had pulled back her hair with a decorative hairpiece and her nail polish matched her eyeshadow. She smiled politely at Mr. Henderson.

"Hi. I'm Savannah from Virginia. I'm a P.G. living in Carrington House."

I had no idea what she meant. Thankfully, I wasn't the only one at the table. Michael screwed up his face in confusion. "What's a P.G.? Party Guest?"

While Michael laughed at his own joke, the rest of us rolled our eyes. I was finding him to be more annoying than my younger brother. Joey was only eleven and had better manners than this kid. Hopefully, he wouldn't be in any of my classes.

Savannah glared at Michael. "P.G. stands for *post graduate*. As in, I graduated from high school in June. In only three years. But I wanted to take a year off before going to college. I'm taking a lot of English electives this term to improve my poetry and polish my portfolio before working on my applications."

Everyone turned to me and I could feel the heat rush to my cheeks. I felt so lowly compared to my new peers. "Uh, hi. I'm Melinda. I'm from here in Connecticut. But the shoreline. It's like, two hours away from here."

I wasn't sure what else I could share. Not that it mattered. At the table beside ours, Sally stood and clapped her hands for attention. The room grew silent as we all turned to face her.

At the next table, Mr. Birkenhead got to his feet. "I hope you are all enjoying your supper! As you may have noticed, dessert is now available. Please help yourselves. You have about half an hour before we need to head to the chapel for the Matriculation Ceremony. When we get there, you may sit where you please, but do *not* use the balcony. While there are no assigned seats, I encourage you to sit beside people you have not yet met, so you may make as many new friends as possible before classes begin this weekend."

He turned to Sally, who smiled at all of us. "Adding to that, I just want to mention one quick rule about the dining hall. You may have noticed the eight tables on the other side of the fireplace. That is the Senior Section and is for sixth formers and invited guests only."

The deans returned to their seats, and conversations slowly resumed throughout the room. I worried Mr. Henderson would want me to continue introducing myself, but he seemed to have forgotten. He spent the rest of the meal asking whether we had settled into our rooms and what we thought of the dorms.

I spent it wondering when this day would be over.

Chapter 12

MR. HENDERSON WAS TELLING US ABOUT THE EIGHT senior girls that lived in his house when Michael interrupted him. "I want to see what they have for dessert."

As rude as he had been, he had a point. Dessert sounded good. Noah, Savannah, and I all excused ourselves to examine the tables.

The buffet stands were gone, replaced with trays of cookies, each the size of my palm. A decorative tower held a display of large yellow cupcakes with a tall stack of black frosting. The end of the table contained individual plates with slices of cheesecake, drizzled with a cherry on top in a thick red sauce.

I took a small plate from the head of the table, selecting a cupcake and chocolate cookie before returning to my seat. As I settled into my chair, Michael pulled the bottom of his cupcake until he had the stem in one hand and the top in the other. I watched as he smashed the bottom onto the top, making frosting ooze from the sides.

He held the mess in front of his face with a smug expression. "It's a sandwich." Before any of us could respond, he shoved the entire dessert into his mouth. It was too much food to fit, so cake crumbs and bits of frosting fell onto the table as he chewed with his mouth open.

Lexi glared at him. "That is disgusting. You're getting that mess on me! Can you at least cover your mouth?"

Jackson nodded. "Really, man. That's just not needed. Maybe at lunch or something. But, come on, man. This is a special dress event. Can't you use some manners?"

Mr. Henderson watched the scene with an amused expression. He was the adult at the table. He should have intervened. But, before I could ask him to, Michael swallowed the cupcake. While the rest of us took turns glaring at the mess, Mr. Henderson glanced at his watch.

"It's getting late. We need to get to the chapel for the Matriculation Ceremony."

As much as I didn't want my new classmates to realize my ignorance, I had heard this word more times than I could count today. And yet, I still didn't know what it meant. I looked directly at Mr. Henderson to avoid my classmates' eyes.

"Um, people keep mentioning this ceremony. But what is it, exactly? I mean, I've never been to one before. What's it all about?"

I could feel my face growing warm, but Noah nodded. "Yeah. I was wondering that myself."

Really? I wasn't the only clueless person at the table? I was so happy, I could scream. Instead, I sent Noah an appreciative smile.

Meanwhile, Mr. Henderson looked like the cat who swallowed the canary. "I can't tell you much because you will have a better experience if you don't know what's coming.

However, think of it as an initiation ceremony. The deans will introduce you to the school and its rules. It is interactive, so you will want to pay close attention in order to take part fully."

Mr. Henderson got to his feet. "Now, it looks as if it is time to leave. Do you all know where to bring your plates?"

Lexi frowned. "No. This is my first meal here."

Noah smiled. "It's okay. I'll show you."

As Mr. Henderson brought his plate to the dishroom, Michael stood. "I want another cupcake before we leave."

Lexi jumped out of her chair. "Eww. I am *not* sitting next to that boy through another cupcake. I'll see you all in the chapel. Um, Noah? Can you show me where to get rid of this?"

Noah nodded. "Yeah. I'm leaving with you."

Everyone agreed. I felt guilty about Michael returning to an empty table, but I couldn't stomach the idea of watching him eat another cupcake in such a disturbing manner.

I also didn't want to walk to the chapel alone. I followed my tablemates to the dish room, placing my plates on the belt and my flatware in the bins before returning to the dining hall.

My classmates hadn't waited for me. I was hurt, but I never actually *asked* them to stay behind. They were probably trying to put as much distance between themselves and Michael. I couldn't blame them for that.

"Hey, Roomie!"

I turned to the familiar voice. Sarah was approaching with another girl. She smiled. "Wait up?"

Of course! She didn't have to ask. When they emerged from the dish room, Sarah gestured to the girl beside her as we followed the rest of our classmates out of the building.

"Jasmine, this is my roommate, Melinda. Melinda, this is Jasmine. She's a day student."

I smiled. "Oh! Is your locker in the MAC?"

Jasmine shook her head. "No. Those are for upper formers. Third formers are in the Stanton basement. Near the deans' offices."

I frowned. "That doesn't sound very comfortable."

"It's not that bad. There's a lounge with snack machines and soda machines."

When we reached the chapel, I held the door for my friends before following them into the building. Although there were three sets of doors, we had entered through the center. On either side of the vast entryway was a curving staircase to the balcony and a straight one to a lower level.

I followed Sarah and Jasmine into the main part of the chapel. Although I attended Mass regularly with my parents, I had only been in Catholic churches and the décor of this new place intrigued me. Large windows with frosted glass lined both sides of the room. Square pillars divided the area into three sections. The balcony was above the outer rows of wooden pews, while chandeliers hung over the center row.

Unlike every church I had ever attended, the benches were white with plush red cushions that ran the length of the seat. Jasmine slid into a row on the right near the front. Sarah sat beside her and I followed. While I waited for the mysterious ceremony to begin, my eyes were drawn to the front of the chapel. The stage was only a step above the rest of the room, its red carpet matching the pew cushions. A small altar table sat against the back wall.

What I found most striking, however, was the multicolored quilted tapestry on the front wall. I wasn't positive what it was supposed to represent, although I was pretty sure I could depict a mountain and a river in the picture.

Just in front of the stage was a folding table upon which sat the largest book I had ever seen. Each page had to be at least as long as my forearm. They were yellowed, suggesting the book was probably older than me, although it was possible someone had antiqued it to look that way. It was also very thick, at least several hundred sheets long, with a wide black and gold ribbon running between the open pages, dangling off the edge of the table in our direction.

As Sally and Mr. Birkenhead walked towards the front of the room, two horrible thoughts crossed my mind at the same time. I finally understood why Mr. Henderson refused to give us the details of the ceremony. The deans were going to read the *entire* book aloud. It would take hours and bore me to tears, probably even putting me to sleep. And then, they would test us on its contents.

But my second thought was even worse. Mr. Henderson had said the ceremony was interactive. What if the deans expected each of us to read from the book? I shuddered at the thought. I hated speaking in public.

Sally and Mr. Birkenhead stood behind the book, and the chapel quickly quieted. It was as if someone had flipped a switch. Sally gazed about the room with a smile.

"Good evening and welcome again. I'm sure you are all eager to learn about tonight's ceremony."

Mr. Birkenhead gestured to the book before him. "This is the Hartfield register. Every student who has ever attended Hartfield has signed this book." He gave a small laugh. "Well, not this actual book. When the school became co-ed, we began this second book."

Sally nodded. "This book is a contract, and your signature means you agree to its terms. You have all read the school handbook and are aware of our strict honor code. The contract states: *On my honor, I pledge to adhere to the high standards of behavior set forth by the Honor Code and that violation of said Honor Code will result in disciplinary action, including dismissal from the Charles and Rachel Hartfield Preparatory Academy for Young Men and Women.*"

I considered that as Sally read the Honor Code from the student handbook. By signing my name in this book, I agreed to follow the Honor Code. Of course, I would never cheat on purpose. But what if I did it by accident? Would they kick me out of the school?

What would happen if I didn't sign the book? Would they still allow me to attend Hartfield?

Did I want to? Although I hadn't forgiven my parents for sending me here against my will, what would they think if I were sent home before classes even began?

The students in the front row formed a line on our side of the book and the first one signed her name. When there were only three people waiting, Mr. Birkenhead called my row to join the queue. It wasn't long before the boy in front of me passed me the pen.

I glanced at the page before me, divided into three columns with today's date in upper right corner. As I signed my name, I couldn't help think about how many signatures were in this book. The number of people who had signed these pages before me. There was so much history, right here, under my fingers. I was taking part in a ceremony that thousands of people before me had done. In this room. In this book. The knowledge filled me with a sense of awe.

Part of me wanted to leaf through the book, read all the names, see what history I could gain from the pages. But people were waiting behind me.

I passed the pen to my roommate and walked back to my seat. When Jasmine returned, she and Sarah held a whispered conversation, but I couldn't participate. I was too busy staring at the book.

As each classmate signed it, I could feel the power binding that person to follow the rules. It was awe-inspiring. I was glad no one had explained the ceremony to me ahead of time. Mr. Henderson was right. This was something I had to experience on my own.

When the last person had signed the book, Sally broke the majesty by reviewing the schedule for the evening. We had about half an hour before our advisors expected us in the common rooms for dorm meetings.

Who knew how long that would take? I certainly didn't want to remain in special dress for that. Maybe if Sally dismissed us quickly enough, I could change into pajamas for the meeting.

But first, she had to explain tomorrow's schedule. In great detail. Seriously? Weren't we capable of reading it ourselves?

Finally, the ceremony ended, and the deans dismissed us. The benefit of sitting in front was that I was among the first students to sign the book this year. The downside was that I was one of the last to get through the bottleneck at the doors to leave the building.

Jasmine followed me and Sarah back to the dorms, disappearing through a side door to Stanton as we continued to Woodward. The bottleneck to get into the dorm wasn't as bad. I had just enough time to change. I couldn't wait to see how boring a dorm meeting would be.

Chapter 13

WHEN I RETURNED TO MY ROOM, I WENT DIRECTLY TO my wardrobe. I needed something comfortable to wear to bed, but nothing that would embarrass me in front of my new housemates. I frowned. Where was everything, anyway?

I opened the first drawer. Underwear. With a sigh, I closed it and checked the next one. Socks and pajamas. Bingo!

Right on top was a set Casey had given me for my last birthday. The bottoms were pink with cute teddy bears on them, with one larger one on the matching tank.

Although they were from the juniors' department, would my classmates think them too babyish? I glanced at Sarah. She was lying on her bed with her computer near her pillow, typing furiously. She didn't see me staring.

She had already changed into blue lounge pants with a monkey pattern. Not only did she have a matching shirt, she was also wearing fluffy monkey slippers.

That was all I needed to see. I quickly changed into the teddy bears. I didn't have matching slippers, but Casey had given me thick pink socks to go with the pajamas. After shoving all my dirty clothes into my new purple laundry bag, I glanced at the clock. I had ten minutes until the meeting.

And I really had to pee. I had no clue where the bathroom was. I hadn't needed to go while I was in the dorm earlier. Actually, I had only used the ones in the theater today, hadn't I? I knew Sarah could probably point me in the right direction, but this felt like a mission I had to accomplish alone.

"I'll meet you downstairs," I called over my shoulder as I stepped into the hall. Without waiting for a response, I turned left, examining the doors as I passed.

The rooms on the other side of the hall only had one apple on each door. Was it possible not everyone had a roommate? As much as I liked Sarah, it would have been nice to have had my own room.

I passed a staircase and a few more bedrooms before reaching the end of the hall. In front of me was a closed door that said *Advisor* on the plaque on the wall. A metal baby gate was in the jamb.

On my right was a room marked *Showers*. This had to be the bathroom. Pushing open the door, I stepped inside.

It was more humid than I expected. The tile wall seemed to be an extension of the mosaic pattern on the floor. The gray partition on my left, which reached almost to the ceiling, gave the claustrophobic feeling of being in a narrow hallway. After walking to the back wall and turning the corner, I could see the rest of the room.

There were no sinks, but six gray stalls on my left, separated by those same partitions. Instead of doors, each had pale pink curtains. Made of a heavy material and reaching to the floor, they hung from a rod at the top of the walls.

I had never seen a bathroom stall without doors. I was hesitant to use the toilet, but did I have any other option? Pushing aside the closest curtain, I peered inside.

There was no toilet. The back half of the stall was a walk-in shower with another curtain. The front part was a changing area with a wooden bench against the wall.

I was glad to have found the showers, but what I really needed was a toilet. Where were they?

With a sigh, I returned to the hallway, passing my room and the other set of stairs before reaching the opposite end. Again, I was facing an advisor's door with a metal gate in the jamb. The apple on my right read *Adrienne.* The plaque to my left said *Bathroom.*

As soon as I entered, I knew I had found the correct room. It looked like a public restroom. To my right was a bank of four sinks with a long mirror behind it. On my left were an equal number of stalls. The kind with doors. I chose the closest one, relieved to find a toilet.

When I entered the common room a few minutes later, I found it about half as full as it had been at our last dorm meeting. Sarah was sitting in a window seat with another girl. As I approached, my roommate shifted slightly, patting the space beside her.

"Melinda. Come sit with us. You'll fit."

It was a tight squeeze, but no one seemed to mind. The girl on Sarah's other side gave a small wave.

"Hi! I'm Jade. You're Sarah's roommate?"

I nodded. "Melinda. Can I just say, I *love* your hair?"

Her long black locks contained chunky highlights in a glittery blue that somehow matched perfectly. Jade smiled, pushing her thin wire glasses higher on her nose. "Thanks. I had to wait until I got here yesterday before doing it. If my mother had seen it, she would have never let me come here."

I frowned. "Yesterday? I thought today was moving day."

"International students came in yesterday. We had a bunch of orientation meetings about our green cards and American laws and everything." She rolled her eyes. "It was *so* boring. Like any of us would come here if we hadn't already learned all that stuff."

I had detected no accent. I had assumed Jade was from the area. I raised my eyebrows. "International? Where are you from?"

"Beijing."

Sarah let out a low whistle. "That had to be a long flight."

"You have no idea. Six hours to Tokyo, not including the one-hour layover in Dalian. Then a twelve-hour overnight to New Jersey. Spent a couple of nights in New York City before coming here yesterday."

And I thought two hours from home was bad. I shook my head slowly. "That's got to be hard. Can I just ask? What's worse? All that traveling? Or having your parents so far away?"

Jade bit her lip. "I miss my *mâmâ*. She's staying in New York for the week, so I can still call her. But my *bàba* is still in Beijing and there's a fourteen-hour time difference, so it is difficult to find a time to call him." She shrugged. "But I couldn't turn down the opportunity to study in America."

Out of the corner of my eye, I saw Sally enter the room. While she spoke with the prefects, still wearing their yellow shirts, I glanced around me. Most of my new housemates had changed into pajamas or other comfortable clothes. Only a few girls were still in their special dress outfits.

The room was noisier than the last time we were all gathered. However, when Sally raised a hand, it quickly quieted, and she smiled at all of us.

"Hello again. We're at a slight disadvantage. You all know who I am, but I've only met some of you. So, if you will humor me, I'm going to take attendance so I can put a face to those names." She held up her tablet. "There are eighty-one of you, so please bear with me. Let's start with the garden level. Melissa? Raise your hand, please?"

The girl in a yellow shirt did as instructed, and Sally pointed to her. "Melissa is your prefect. She is in room G1, across from the bathroom. You are welcome to visit her if you have any questions or concerns. Okay. So, beginning with room G1, Alexia Davis?"

It didn't surprise me to see my dinner tablemate, Lexi, raised her hand. Sally scanned the room, nodding at her before returning to her tablet. She called seventeen more names on the garden level. I didn't recognize any of the girls.

Or any of the eighteen people on the first floor. By the time she got to my level, I had zoned out. I felt Sarah raise her hand.

Our dean nodded. "And Melinda Luzzelli?"

I raised my hand. Sally smiled. "Yes. We met this morning. I thought I saw you hiding over there."

Sally had remembered me? I was amazed. Had she remembered anyone else?

I decided to pay better attention as names were called. I had already missed 211.

"Room 212. Jessica Swanson?"

I saw a hand go into the air from the other side of a couch, but I couldn't see the girl who owned it. "Jessi."

"Nice to meet you, Jessi." Sally frowned at her tablet. "I'm going to need some help on this one. You-She Shway?"

Jade raised her hand with a giggle. "Close. The family name goes first. Xué Yù-shí. My name translates to *Jadestone*, so please call me *Jade*."

Sally made a note on her tablet with a nod. "Jade. Yes. We met yesterday."

It took half an hour for our dean to complete the roll call. She wouldn't do this every dorm meeting, would she? As Sally was finishing the third floor, a man and woman entered the room. The dean smiled at them.

"Perfect timing." She turned back to us. "As you are probably aware, I live on the south side of the building." She pointed toward the bathrooms. "I have entrances on every floor except the third. If my door is closed, please feel free to open it and shout inside or visit me on another level." She gestured to the man and woman. "Would you like to introduce yourselves?"

Seriously? We had to do that entire roll call *again*? No, we didn't. Sally hadn't been speaking to us. She had been looking at the other adults.

The woman spoke first. "Welcome, ladies. My name is Clarissa Price, but you may call me Clarissa. This is my husband, David. We live on the north side of the building." She pointed toward the showers. "Our doors are on the first, second, and third floors. What else? I teach history and David teaches English. We share an office on the second floor of the Humanities building."

I leaned closer to Sarah, my voice barely a whisper. "What does that mean?"

Her response was equally quiet. "It's the building on the other side of the boys' dorm. There's like, English and history and religion and classes like that."

I was still confused, but I nodded and turned my attention back to Clarissa.

"We have two children: Molly is four and Tommy is one." She turned to her husband. "Did I forget anything?"

He shrugged. "You're welcome to visit during office hours or try to find us in the dorm. Even if it's the middle of the night."

Sally nodded. "And that's the perfect transition into dorm rules."

"And my cue to leave. Goodnight, ladies." With a wave, Mr. Price disappeared down the hallway.

As Clarissa moved near Sally, the dean smiled at us. "Let's begin by discussing personal property. For many of you, this might be the first time you have had to share your living space with others. I ask that you please respect each other's personal property. I would also discourage you from leaving things in public spaces, such as the bathrooms or showers, as it quickly leads to clutter."

Clarissa nodded. "We also ask that you keep the volume on your music and computers at a reasonable level. If you must break your eardrums, please do so with headphones." She paused as we all giggled. "This is especially important during study hours. Uh, Bethany? Want to explain what that is?"

A prefect stepped forward. "Sure. So, basically, every night is a school night. Except Saturday, but we'll talk about that later. You need to be in the dorm by 7:30 and study with your door open. Like Clarissa said. You can listen to music or whatever, but you need to have headphones on. The music ensembles—orchestra, chorus, theater? They usually have rehearsal during first study hours. Some of the clubs meet then, too. If you're doing that, you just need to let Clarissa or Sally know that's where you're going to be."

Clarissa smiled. "You can also study in the library or meet with a teacher. Again, you need to let me or Sally know where you will be and check in when you return."

Sally nodded. "First study hours ends at 9:00. During the break, you can grab a snack at the MAC or visit with friends. At 9:45, study hours resume and you must all be in the dorm. No exceptions. Lights out is at 10:45, although you may ask your prefect for more time if you are working on an assignment. Saturdays, you must be in the dorms by 11:30. Lights out is at midnight."

Seriously? A bedtime? I glanced around. Most of the girls looked as frustrated as I felt. I hadn't had a bedtime since I was five.

But that wasn't the end of the rules. Sally spoke a little louder to drown out everyone who was groaning.

"Boys are not permitted in the dorm during the class day. They can be in the common room after classes and during the break between study hours. If you would like a boy to visit in your room, you must request *co-ed* from me or one of the Prices."

Clarissa raised a finger. "Me or David. Getting permission from Molly does not count."

I giggled, but I was among the few. A lot of the girls looked upset by this rule. I couldn't understand why. Who wanted boys in their room, anyway?

Sally gave a small nod. "If you have received co-ed permission, you must keep the door open and the light on." She turned to the prefects. "You sixth-formers, as I'm sure you know, may close your doors provided your guest is also a sixth-former."

I knew the co-ed rule was more for the prefects than for us third formers. We were too young for adult relationships. Being with a boy meant maybe holding his hand. Possibly a kiss on the cheek.

But the girls around me were still grumbling. Someone on the floor raised her hand. "What about siblings? Do I need co-ed if my brother wants to hang out in my room?"

Sally nodded. "Yes. But getting co-ed is not a big deal. We just want to know when there are boys in the dorm. We will almost always grant you permission."

Another girl spoke up. "When wouldn't you?"

Sally frowned. "Sometimes when it is too close to study hours. Or one of you is having disciplinary problems. Your roommate may have asked not to have the boy in the room."

Several girls glared at each other. Even Sarah sent me a look of warning, although she was smiling, so I wasn't sure how much she meant it.

The meeting continued forever. Our advisors had rules for everything. When we could leave campus, where we could go, and how we were permitted to get there. When we were allowed to leave the dorm in the morning and when we had to return in the evening. What we could have in our rooms and what was forbidden.

Finally, the meeting ended. I thought my head might explode from everything I had learned about my new home.

Although a few girls stopped to talk to Sally, Clarissa, or a prefect, most of us returned to our rooms. Of course, this created a traffic jam in the hallway and stairwell.

As soon as I reached my room, I grabbed my shower basket and rushed down the hall. I wanted to be in and out of the bathroom before the rest of the girls on my floor realized all of us were sharing just four stalls. Only one person had beaten me there. As I brushed my teeth, I made a mental note to buy a second basket for things that required a sink, like my toothbrush and toothpaste.

After brushing too quickly to have any effect on potential cavities, I headed to a stall. A handful of girls entered, carrying baskets similar to mine. The volume of the bathroom increased as more people arrived. There was so much noise, it felt as if every girl on the floor, maybe even some from the first or third floor as well, were jammed into the small space.

From within the sanctuary of my stall, I heard someone call out, her tone full of disgust. "What is *that*?"

Sarah was definitely the voice that responded. "What? You've never seen OxiClear before?"

How could she not? The commercials were everywhere. I exited the stall in time to see someone sending my roommate an incredulous look.

"Yeah, I've seen it. I've just never seen anyone use that much of it before."

With a shrug, Sarah continued to slather the white cream over her face, stepping backward to allow me to wash my hands in her sink. I left the water running for my roommate to rinse her face, grabbed my basket, and fled from the room. The hallway was blissfully quiet.

It wasn't very late, but I was exhausted. Leaving the light for Sarah, I crawled into bed. I set the alarm on my phone early enough to shower and have breakfast before my first meeting. There were several messages waiting for me, but I was too tired to deal with them.

Clutching Bonnie beneath the covers, I rolled over to face the wall. Sarah walked in a moment later, but I closed my eyes and pretended to be asleep. I could tell she was making an effort to be quiet as she got ready for bed and turned off the lights.

As tired as I was, I wasn't sure I would ever fall asleep. My mind was turning over everything that had happened today. This morning, I had awoken in my own room at home. During the last twelve or so hours, I had met at least a hundred people and had more rules thrown at me than I would ever remember. How many times had I sung the school song? Would I dream of it tonight?

Chapter 14

FRIDAY MORNING, THE GENTLE BUZZING SOUND OF my phone woke me. I was on my stomach, my arms hugging my pillow. I reached for my phone on my nightstand.

Except it wasn't on my nightstand. It was on my desk. Because I wasn't home. I was at my new school.

I rolled out of bed, picking up Bonnie from the floor. One day, I would get through the night without throwing my beloved friend on the floor in my sleep. Using the morning sunlight to see, I straightened my sheets and comforter to make my bed, setting Bonnie to stand guard in the center.

I winced at the creaking noise the wardrobe doors made as I opened them. But a quick glance over my shoulder reassured me that Sarah hadn't stirred. As quietly as possible, I pulled open the bottom drawer and selected a pair of denim shorts. After removing a purple top from a hanger, I grabbed underwear from the top drawer and tossed everything on the bed.

In the space between my wardrobe and bed, I had lined my shoes under the edge of the bed. I slipped on my black flip-flops before pulling my towel from the hook on the side of the wardrobe. After grabbing my shower basket, I closed the closet, again wincing at the creak. I would have to ask Sally or Adrienne what I could do about the noise.

Gathering my things, I crept out of my room and tiptoed down the hallway to the bathroom. After brushing my teeth and using the toilet, I again collected my things and trekked down the hall to the shower room. Who had designed this dorm? Why couldn't there be a single bathroom on each floor?

Shaking my head at the inconvenience of the situation, I couldn't help noticing the stillness of my floor. No one was awake. It was simply too quiet. I couldn't even hear any music playing.

No one had been in the bathroom. I had the shower room to myself as well. Choosing a random stall, I dumped my belongings onto the bench and closed the pink curtain behind me.

I stared at my things. I would need a better organizational system. The shower had a built-in shelf large enough for my shampoo, conditioner, body wash, and facial cleanser. I hung my poofie on the knob.

There were several hooks on the walls. I placed my towel on one and my clothes on the other. Finally, I kicked my shoes under the bench and turned on the shower.

While the water warmed, I removed my clothes, folding them roughly and placing them on the bench before stepping into the shower.

I let the warm water engulf me. I had needed this. Yesterday had been very trying. Today was bound to be just as bad. Probably worse, because I had meetings scheduled until dinner time. How was I going to make it through the day?

After my shower, I quickly dressed, placing my soaps in my basket and making sure I had all my things before exiting the stall. When I returned to my room, I realized I didn't want to store my wet shower things in my wardrobe after all. But it fit on the floor in front of my dance bag. Maybe I could buy a boot tray for underneath it.

I tossed my dirty clothes into my laundry bag and grabbed my phone. After checking I had my key, I snuck out of my room, quiet as a mouse. As I exited the dorm, I tried to remember the square I had drawn on my mental map of the campus. I turned right and headed to the main road. By the time I was ready to cross, I could see the dining hall.

Breakfast was not a very popular meal. The senior section was empty. I encountered no one from the time I left my room to time I grabbed a tray. The only people in the servery were the cafeteria workers.

I examined my options. I could always get something from the cereal bar. A waffle iron stood just behind the counter, so I assumed someone would make me one if I wanted. Turning slightly, I saw two women beside the griddle. On the counter behind them were several large trays of eggs.

Before deciding what to eat, I explored the other side of the servery. The pasta bar had transformed into a breakfast bar with pancakes, syrups, strawberries in sauce, oatmeal, and a mushy substance that looked like the grits I had once seen in a television show.

But I was more fascinated by the contraption that had replaced yesterday's pizza bar. It was a metal box with two large holes in the front. A man—probably a teacher—stood before it, slicing an English muffin on his plate. I watched him place the bread in the top slot and fiddle with the control knobs as the wire conveyor slowly slid the English muffin to the rear of the machine. When it reached the back and fell off the belt, I thought the man had lost his breakfast and would have to start again. But the toast had slid into the bottom slot beneath the wire conveyor.

I had to play with this machine. I had never seen a toaster like this, not even on television. The bread selection beside it was enormous. As the man walked away with his food, I stared at my options. Everything sounded good, but I wasn't much of a breakfast person.

Finally, I settled on a raisin bagel. I was able to pull apart the two halves without a knife. Examining the dials, I set the darkness to light and the speed to medium before placing the bagel face-up on the belt. I almost giggled as the machine ate my food and fell down the back. I also nearly burned my hands trying to remove the toast from the front.

There was a stack of plates beside the machine. I tossed my breakfast onto the top one before placing the plate on my tray. Cream cheese would go well with this. With a frown, I glanced around. I didn't see any. Or butter. Or jelly or peanut butter or any other toppings.

But I had seen the salad bar near the fireplace. Maybe the peanut butter was there. After grabbing a glass of orange juice from the beverage island, I went to check. Sure enough, the salad bar had peanut butter. But it also had cream cheese.

I turned to the dining hall. The man I had seen at the toaster was sitting in the smaller section with a woman and three young children. He was offering toast to the girl in a booster seat, but she seemed more interested in throwing the bread at her brother than eating it.

There was no one else in the dining hall. I settled myself for a table along the half-wall, about halfway between the servery and the rear wall. As I bit into my bagel, I checked my phone. Brittany and Casey were looking for me in a group text we often shared. When I didn't respond, both had sent me private messages asking if I was ignoring them on purpose.

Brittany had texted me after school, complaining of boredom and wishing I could meet her at the shopping plaza. Casey had texted me at night, hoping I could watch her favorite reality show with her.

It was something we often did on Thursday nights. Although I didn't love the show, I enjoyed talking to my friend as we watched it, making fun of the contestants. But I had completely forgotten about television last night. How was that even possible?

With a sigh, I realized I may never find time to watch my favorite shows. Most were on during study hours. I would have to watch them on-demand and, if yesterday was any indication, I wasn't sure if I would ever have the time.

Instead of repeating myself, I used the group text to respond to Brittany and Casey. I told them a little about Hartfield and moving into the dorm. About having a roommate and having to buy textbooks. About my parents abandoning me and formal dinners. About the dorm meeting that ran so late, I had no energy do to anything but crash.

I left out the part about having a bedtime. It felt ridiculous to admit it. But I shared some of the other rules, such as required study times and no televisions. Just in case they didn't get the hint, I spelled out that I wouldn't be able to watch our favorite shows together anymore. After telling them

I would probably be too busy to answer their texts again today, I promised to keep my phone charged so we could talk tomorrow.

We all knew I would forget to charge my phone, but I could promise anyway. I told them I missed them before putting away my phone. I reached for my bagel, but it was missing. How had I eaten the entire thing?

While I finished my juice, I reviewed the mint green *Daily Docket*. My first meeting began at ten and, although there were some breaks, didn't end until the Convocation ceremony following dinner. After that would be study hours.

What exactly was I supposed to study? I hadn't attended any classes yet. Was there some summer assignment I needed to complete?

Glancing up, I could see a few more people in the dining hall. Some seniors in yellow shirts were sitting in their special section. A few families and random adults. A few other people who looked as lost as I felt.

I brought my tray to the dish room, but I didn't want to walk through the senior section with all those students there. I opted for the side exit I had seen Sarah use yesterday.

Passing through the door, I found myself in a stairwell. Upstairs was probably the dorms Sarah had mentioned yesterday. I went downstairs, finding the exit easily.

When I emerged outside, though, it took a moment for me to get my bearings. I could see the bridge between the dining hall and library. I was behind the buildings. And, I could see the main road. As I approached it, I could see that Humanities place across the street. My dorm should be just beyond that. I walked along the sidewalk to the front of the building, breathing a mental sigh of relief when I recognized my surroundings. Maybe I was getting the hang of things after all.

Woodward was still quiet when I returned. Although I could hear a shower running on the first floor as headed up the staircase, there was no music or conversation. When I snuck into my room, Sarah was still asleep.

I didn't want to wake her, so went to the common room, curling up in one of the window seats and reading through random social media feeds. Gradually, the noise in the room increased as the dorm slowly awoke. Every so often, I would see girls making their way to the bathroom or shower. Others were heading out in small groups, probably in search of breakfast.

Eventually, I glanced at the time. It was only half an hour before our first meeting. When I returned to my room, Sarah was awake and dressed, playing with her computer on her bed.

She turned as I closed the door behind me. "Hey, you. Where'd you disappear to?"

I shrugged. "Couldn't sleep. Went for breakfast, then hung out down in the common room."

"Ooh. Breakfast! Thanks for the reminder." Withing unfolding her legs, Sarah reached under her bed, pulling out a plastic bin. Her hair fell to the floor, so I couldn't see what she was doing, but a moment later, she pushed the bin back under her bed and sat up. In her hand was a protein bar. I giggled as she held it up for me to see.

Rolling my eyes, I gestured to the door. "Ready for an endless day of orientation?"

Sarah jumped off the bed. "Let's go!"

Following her out of the dorm, I wished I had her enthusiasm. Personally, I was not looking forward to the day.

Chapter 15

TODAY'S MEETINGS WERE SCHEDULED TO BEGIN IN the VAPAC theater. Sarah and I sat in roughly the same seats as we had yesterday. We didn't have to wait long for Mr. Birkenhead to step behind the podium.

"Good morning. How was everyone's first night at Hartfield?"

There were several enthusiastic responses before he held up a hand for silence.

"I'm glad to hear you are all adjusting to your new homes. This morning, we will divide into groups. The senior leading your group will be your guide for the morning. After lunch, you will have your first form meetings. Please listen for your prefect's name. I'm going to start with day students."

There were a lot of day student prefects. Mr. Birkenhead called about eight before naming an orientation leader. After day students, he went through the new upper formers, again reading several prefect names before assigning a leader. Eventually, he reached my dorm.

"Girls in Woodward with Adrienne as your prefect. If you are in rooms 201 through 208, you will be with Sophia. If you are in rooms 209 through 215, you will be with Trinity."

I didn't pay attention as he finished the dorms. A moment later, he dismissed us to find our leaders in the courtyard.

Even though there was a mass of people, it wasn't difficult to spot Trinity. In addition to her bright yellow shirt, she was holding a sheet of posterboard above her head with her name on it.

As we gathered around our leader, Sarah immediately started talking to a boy that had been in the summer program with her, and Jade joined in. I didn't. I was too busy wondering what Trinity's actual hair color might be, since I was fairly certain she had not been born with hair the color of a leprechaun. It looked odd against her ivory skin.

Trinity did a few headcounts before reaching whatever number she was expecting. Rolling her poster into a cone, she put it to her lips and shouted.

"Okay. Trinity's group! We're on the move!"

She returned the sign above her head as she made her way up the concrete steps. We were a big blob behind her.

I had not been to this part of campus. There was a vast field behind the VAPAC before the path went uphill. More buildings stood at the base and top of the hill.

Trinity marched to the middle of the lawn before halting. We all gathered around expectantly. Our leader placed her sign on the ground and smiled at us.

"Good morning! As you've probably guessed, I'm Trinity and I'm going to be helping you all today. The first thing we're going to do is get in a circle so we can all see each other."

There had to be a couple dozen of us, so our circle took a moment to form. Eventually, we were standing shoulder to shoulder, and Trinity nodded.

"Great. Now, everyone sit where you are. We're going to introduce ourselves, but I don't want you to just tell me your name. You have to think of one word to describe yourself."

I bit my lip. How could I describe myself in one word? Scared? Homesick? Confused? Overwhelmed?

Trinity hadn't finished her rules, though. "Here's the catch. The word has to start with the same letter as your first initial. We'll go around the circle. I'll start. I'm Temperamental Trinity." She pointed to the boy beside her. "What's your name?"

Slowly, we made our way around the circle, and Trinity smiled mischievously. "Great job, you guys. Okay. Now it's time for our first game. We're going to do this again, but when it's your turn, you have to introduce yourself, as well as the people sitting on either side of you."

I glanced around the circle. Most people looked as scared as I felt. Trinity ignored our fear.

"So, hi again. I'm Temperamental Trinity. This is Kooky Katy and Wacky Walter."

Wacky Walter introduced Temperamental Trinity and Jumpy Jade. She introduced Wacky Walter and Silly Sarah. After my roommate introduced Jumpy Jade and me, it was my turn.

I took a deep breath. "Um, I'm Mellow Melinda." I pointed to my right. "This is Silly Sarah." I turned to the girl on my left. Wasn't her name Allison? But what was the other part? "And this is, uh, this is Artsy Allison?"

As Artsy Allison introduced herself, I vowed to pay closer attention to the names in case the next task was even more challenging. However, after Kooky Katy finished, Trinity got to her feet.

"Alrighty. New game. Everybody up, but stay in the circle." She gave us a moment to stand. "Now, raise your right hand. Your other right hand, Awesome Andy. There you go. Okay. Now, move a little closer and put your right hand into the center of the circle."

She took a step backward as we all followed her instructions. "Great. Now, grab the hand of the person across from you. Or close to it."

Someone squeezed my fingers. I looked around, but I couldn't see my own hand. Even though I had no idea who was holding it, I tightened my grip.

Trinity smiled. "Everyone have a hand? Great. Now. Keep holding that hand and reach in with your left hand. Again, try to grab the one across from you."

Someone took my left hand. And I almost lost my balance. But strangers were holding me so tightly, I couldn't reach out to steady myself. I shifted my feet, hoping Trinity would explain why we were doing this.

"Okay. Here's the fun part. Untangle yourselves. *Without letting go.* Work together. Talk to each other. And . . . go!"

A bunch of people immediately started talking. Some shouted directions. Some were trying to figure out who was holding their hands. Some complained that they were in pain.

One of the boys shouted above everyone else. I recognized him as Awesome Andy. "Let's start at the top. You two holding hands on top. Raise them in the air."

The rest of us quieted as two people lifted their left hands a few inches.

Andy nodded. "Great. Okay. So, you in the pink stand still and you in the green move about three people over."

The guy in the green shirt raised his eyebrows. "How?"

"No idea."

With a shrug, the guy tried to push past the person on his right, but Kooky Katy screamed.

"Ow! No! Stop. You can't do that. You nearly broke my arm. This isn't going to work."

Beside me, Sarah frowned, squatting to peer under the knot. "Hey. I think I'm on the bottom here. I can probably crawl under. Then whoever's next on the bottom can follow me."

Andy nodded. "It's worth a shot."

Sarah crawled under the pile, then a few more people followed. Eventually, someone nearly broke an arm trying. But Katy was now free to move closer to the guy in the green shirt.

About fifteen minutes later, we had untied the knot. I was holding hands with Jade's roommate—Jessi—and a boy named Larry. Larry was holding Andy's hand. Andy was holding Jessi's hand. The four of us had made our own little circle while everyone else was in the giant one.

After we all had a good laugh about the situation, Trinity led us to the building at the base of the hill. There was a complex network of paths that led in all directions. Some led up the hill. Some led around the lawn. Some led away toward the main road.

To our left was a stream. I had passed it when coming to the VAPAC from my dorm. On one side of that path, the water ran into pipes to be carried under the main road. On the other side, the stream was dammed, causing the river to form a small pond.

A point near the middle narrowed enough for a small footbridge to cross it. More brick buildings surrounded the pond and an intricate network of paths seemed to connect them all.

Trinity led us toward the nearest building. Nestled on our side of the pond, it was, of course, made of brick. But it didn't look like my dorm. The inside of its U-shape was two stories of glass, slanted to make the first floor wider than the second. Looking up, I saw smaller windows on the top of the building. A third story that almost felt like someone had placed it as an afterthought. A bridge extended over the pond, connecting the second story of the building to the path near the footbridge.

The edges of the U both had glass doors on the first floor. Trinity led us to the pondside one, speaking into her posterboard cone as we walked.

"This is the Science Center. Most of you will have classes in here this year. Your form meetings will almost always be in Baker Auditorium. That's where we're going now. You won't have assigned seats, but for this meeting, please sit in the front two rows on the left."

Trinity opened the door and led the way inside. I looked around in amazement. I had never been in a building like this. The second level was a balcony that came out just about to the glass, and the linoleum floors made everything echo. The long, curved walls opposite the window contained a giant painting depicting the view of Earth as seen from space.

The auditorium was directly in front of us. Just before entering, I thought I heard the clicking sound of a dog's nails on the floor and the jingle of a collar. But that was ridiculous, right?

When Trinity said we were going to an auditorium, I had assumed it would be like the one in my middle school. A theater with a small stage and uncomfortable wooden seats that folded when not in use.

Baker looked more like the council chambers on *NeoGenesis*. The circular room sloped down to a round area at the bottom, where our deans were speaking with a man near a podium. Every few steps, a long desk curved around the room on either side of the aisle, with cushy red executive chairs evenly spaced along them.

There was plenty of room for my entire class, most of whom were already present. Trinity led us to the bottom of the room, indicating where we should look for seats. I was on an end beside Sarah and was still settling into my chair when Sally introduced the guest speaker.

This meeting was about technology. The specialist told us how to connect our computers and phones to the Hartfield Wi-Fi. Although there were different networks around campus, they all used the same password. This term it was *H@rtfie!d*. The specialist gave us a few minutes to enter this into our phones.

The guest speaker then displayed a map of Hartfield, pointing out all the computer labs on campus. Since I still didn't know what half these buildings were, most of his speech went over my head. He followed this with a long lecture about what we were and weren't allowed to do while on the public computers. Since half of what he was listing was illegal, I wasn't sure why it was necessary to mention it.

I stopped listening. The rest of our meetings today wouldn't be this boring, would they?

Chapter 16

AFTER THE MEETING, THE DEANS DISMISSED US BY our orientation groups. Mine was among the last to leave. As we made our way outside, I could see my new classmates heading in various directions. Some went upstairs. Others took paths up the hill or across the pond. Trinity led our group straight to the VAPAC.

At first, I thought we were heading back to the theater, but Trinity opened a door I hadn't noticed earlier. It was tucked between the glass theater entrance and the concrete stairs.

We were in a stairwell and followed Trinity downstairs into a square room unlike any I had ever seen before. One wall contained a bank of mirrors, like a dance studio but without a ballet barre. There was an open door on the other side of the room. Otherwise, the windowless space was completely black. The ceiling. The walls. The floor.

In the center, a chair sat in front of a white backdrop. It was facing a folding table, where a man was sitting with a laptop and a small device that might have been a printer. He stood as we entered.

"Good morning. I'm here to help you set up your student IDs today. It will serve as your library card, your campus debit card, a passkey for certain doors, and your ID for school functions and the off-campus shuttle. In short, don't lose it."

We gave a collective weak laugh before the man continued.

"Please line up along the mirrors and I will call you one at a time. This should go quickly, but I've been having some network issues this morning, so please bear with me."

I was one of the first people called, after Sarah and the girl across the hall whose name I kept forgetting. When it was my turn, I sat in the chair and faced the man. He held a small camera near the top of his computer.

"Say cheese."

I was aware of everyone in my group looking at me and could only manage a weak smile. The man nodded, returning the camera to the table before typing on his computer for a moment.

"All set. Your ID will be ready in a minute. Christina?"

I was going to stand by my roommate when I realized I was thirsty. It had been a long morning. I tried to remember the last time I had seen a water fountain, but I couldn't recall any.

Frowning, I made my way to Trinity, who was studying something on her phone. She looked up as I approached.

"Everything okay?"

I nodded. "Yeah. I was thirsty and was wondering if there was any water nearby."

"Oh, yeah. Sure." She pointed to the door opposite where we had entered. "So, if you go out that way. At the end of the hall, turn left. At the end of the hall is a door. Go upstairs and turn right and—" She sighed. "I'll just show you myself. Come on."

I followed Trinity through hallways lined with collages of musicals performed at the school over the past seventy years. As she twisted and turned through the building, I was glad she had volunteered to lead me.

We went up a staircase, emerging into a well-lit area. After passing the restrooms, Trinity turned a corner, and I saw a water fountain tucked into a small space between some bookcases and a glass partition.

I stared through it. Even though we had entered the VAPAC on the theater side, we were now standing in the gallery side. How was that possible?

I could see students receiving their registration packets. Probably the returning fourth and fifth formers, if I remembered the schedule correctly. Beyond them, I could see the outdoor staircase and door we had used to enter the building.

Trinity squeezed past me to drink from the fountain. Oh yeah. That was why we were here in the first place. After getting a drink myself, I pointed over my shoulder as I followed my guide back downstairs.

"Uh, Trinity?"

"Yeah?"

"The room we're going back to?"

"The black box?"

I sent her a confused look. "The what?"

"The black box. It's one of the dance studios, among other things."

It was a fitting name. I nodded. "Yeah. Well, is it *under* that concrete staircase outside?"

Trinity stopped in the middle of the hall, sending me a look of amusement. "When I was a third former, I took dance as my sport. I spent every day in the black box. And it took me at least two weeks before I realized it was under the stairs."

Shaking her head at the memory, Trinity continued to the black box. Most of my classmates had their IDs in their hands. After the man distributed the last few, Trinity led us back out the door we had entered. Weaving around the returning students, we went to the top of the staircase. We gathered on the lawn beside the theater, and Trinity again turned her poster into a megaphone.

"We don't have time for a full tour, so I'm going to give you the brief one. First of all, did you all get your textbooks?"

Nodding, I looked around. Everyone else was nodding as well. Trinity smiled.

"Perfect. That's the MAC. That's where you'll find the school store and mail room. It's also a great place to relax. Up in the loft is the MAC Attack snack bar."

Trinity took a step back, pointing across the street. "The building behind it, you can kind of see it from here? That's the athletic center, otherwise known as the TRAC. You should go check it out when you get some free time. There's a lot to do there."

Turning, Trinity pointed to the top of the hill. I followed her gaze. It was the strangest building I had ever seen.

When I was younger, my brother and I built a castle using plastic bricks. We made a series of rooms, then assembled them into a tower. This building looked as if it had built the same way. Constructed of large, brown stone blocks, it was too big to be called bricks. Each room held windows that looked larger than me, even from this distance, and they seemed to be stacked at angles to each other. The ones on the lower level jutted straight into the hill while those above it rested on their roofs, extending even further uphill.

Trinity was still talking. "That weird building there? That's the language building. I really wish we had time to go find all your classrooms, because the numbers are really messed up. Please, please, please try to get there today and look for your classes. Don't wait until you're late for your language tomorrow."

Trinity headed along the path to the Science Center, turning to yell through her megaphone. "Beyond the language building are a ton of buildings you don't need to worry about right now."

As we approached the pond, Trinity pointed to her left, our right. "We already went to Science Center. Room numbers are simple. First floor is one hundreds, second floor is two hundreds."

Trinity led us over the footbridge, pointing to the brick and white building on the opposite side of the pond. "This is the infirmary. There are some administrative offices upstairs."

As we continued up along the paths, Trinity pointed out the upper form houses and dorms on both sides of the street. After crossing diagonally at the four-way intersection, Trinity pointed to the third-form dorms, reminding us that our English and history classes would be in Humanities Hall beside it. After pointing out the library, she gestured to the building next to the dining hall.

"That's Johnson. That's where you'll have your math classes. Of course, you all know Hartfield Hall behind you. Uh, let's see. You were in the chapel last night. I think that's all the major buildings. Any of the rest are probably dorms or faculty houses."

Trinity pointed up the enormous staircase. "This is where I leave you. The dining hall should be open. If you have any questions, look for someone in one of these shirts."

As she waved, most of my classmates turned. I followed them into the building with a sigh. The day had only just begun. I had plenty more after lunch. Would today ever end?

OUR AFTERNOON MEETINGS AGAIN STARTED IN THE main theater. Even though I felt like I had made no new friends besides my roommate, I got the impression most of my classmates didn't feel the same. The theater was definitely louder than it had been at previous meetings. Mr. Birkenhead had to tap the microphone with his finger for silence.

The first presentation was by the Director of Health Services. She mentioned a lot of things I had never considered. Now that I was living at Hartfield, if I didn't feel well when I woke up, my mother couldn't call me into school sick. Instead, I would have to contact an advisor who would decide if I needed to visit the infirmary.

If I injured myself, I may not need to go to the hospital. According to the director, our infirmary was better equipped and better staffed than the closest walk-in center. She also described a variety of services available, including nutritional counseling. This led to a long discussion about eating properly.

"Many of you are used to a parent preparing your meals. You probably eat whatever they serve you without thinking about its nutritional content."

She was right. I did. I tried to pay closer attention so I could follow her advice.

"As you have already experienced, you have several options available to you at each meal. I encourage you to think about what you are eating. While pasta might be a nice dinner once in a while, eating it every meal for weeks at a time will cause nutritional deficiencies. If you find you are having difficulties making healthy choices, visit us at the infirmary. We also encourage you to come talk to us if you notice any symptoms of depression."

After telling us how to recognize the signs, she then gave a list of causes, including stress and homesickness. I tried to pay attention, but the lecture was making me drowsy.

It lasted nearly an hour. By the time the director finished, I was ready for a nap. Or at least a snack. Unfortunately, I had to attend our first form meeting.

After the sea of third formers migrated from the VAPAC to Baker Auditorium, it took a moment for us to settle. Finally, we quieted enough for Sally to speak.

"Welcome to your first form meeting. By now, you should have all moved into your dormitories and received your textbooks. If you have any issues with your class schedules or room, please see me or Mr. Birkenhead after the meeting. For now, I'm going to turn things over to Mr. Tucci."

A short, balding man stepped to the podium with a nod. "Good afternoon. I'm Brian Tucci and I'm a college counselor here at Hartfield."

I raised my eyebrows. We hadn't even started our freshman year, and they already expected us to think about college?

"But today I'm here to talk to you about your study habits. Where are some places you like to do your homework?"

Since he was looking at us expectantly, I assumed we needed to answer. I thought about it. Most of the time, I finished my homework on the bus. Something told me that wasn't the answer he was looking for.

Mr. Tucci pointed to someone on the other side of the hall. A girl from my dorm answered.

"I like to study in my room."

Mr. Tucci nodded. "Good, but where? At a desk?"

"Oh. Yeah. I usually work at my desk."

"Good. How about you?" He pointed to a girl in front of me.

"I study in my room, but usually on my bed."

Mr. Tucci nodded. "We're going to talk more about that in a minute."

He pointed to a few more students. My classmates liked to do their homework on the floor and in the library. Some liked to study with friends while others preferred working alone.

I had never really considered it before, but as I listened to my classmates, I realized that preferred to work alone on my bed.

After my class had given several examples, Mr. Tucci smiled at us. "Now, some of those are great places to study, others not so great. Anyone want to guess the worst one you mentioned?"

He looked around, but no one volunteered. I had a feeling I knew what he was going to say.

"Can anyone guess why your bed might not be the best place to study? What else do you do on your bed?"

There were a few snickers, but several people raised their hands. Mr. Tucci pointed to someone in the front row.

"Sleep?"

Mr. Tucci smiled. "Yes. So, if you study and sleep in the same place, one of two things will happen. Either you will train your body to fall asleep while you are studying or you will train your body to stay awake when you are on your bed."

I frowned. He was probably right. But I doubted the floor or my desk would be nearly as comfortable as my bed.

Mr. Tucci wasn't done. He went into a long lecture about consistency, stressing the importance of studying at the same time every day. I didn't see the point. We were already being told we had to study during study hours, which was at the same time every day.

I didn't realize my mind had wandered until I saw my classmates standing. Was our meeting already over?

No. No one was leaving, and Mr. Tucci was still speaking. I quickly got to my feet and listened to the directions.

"Keep your body facing me, but turn your head over your left shoulder. Try to turn as far as possible."

How did this have anything to do with studying? Not really understanding the point, I followed his instructions.

"Good. Turn back to me. Now, close your eyes. I want you to imagine yourself turning as far as you just did. Now, imagine yourself going a little further."

I still didn't understand the point, but I pictured myself turning my head completely around to face him again.

"Good. Now, open your eyes and try to turn your head again." After giving us a minute to do as he said, he had us all sit down. "Raise your hand if you were able to turn to where you saw in your mind."

That was physically impossible. It surprised me to see many of my classmates raising their hands. Was I the only one capable of imagining a revolving head?

I felt like I had missed something important. I tried to pay closer attention, but it didn't make a difference. Mr. Tucci had finished his lecture. After a few closing remarks, he disappeared through a door in the back of the room and Mr. Birkenhead stepped to the podium.

The dean spent a few minutes discussing our student government. Hartfield's student council didn't sound that different from my middle school. I had represented my homeroom in seventh grade. When I was first elected, I was excited to make a difference in our school. When my fellow representatives spent our entire first meeting planning a party—for themselves, not the school—I quickly learned that it was mostly a popularity contest and I wasn't part of their crowd.

Mr. Birkenhead's description gave the impression that our student representative would serve as a bridge between our class and the deans. The position almost sounded tempting. But not enough to make me want to run.

Hartfield had a second student government. The way Mr. Birkenhead described it, the Honor Board was a court where its members decided the fate of anyone suspected of violating the Honor Code. There were two representatives from each form, and they had the power to expel students if the crime was severe enough. Although it was appealing, it sounded like too much responsibility for me.

As Mr. Birkenhead stepped away from the podium, I prepared to leave. However, Sally replaced him. I groaned inwardly. Would this meeting ever end?

Sally pressed something on the podium, and an image appeared on the wall behind her. It was a list of sports. She pointed to it.

"As you know, all students are required to take a sport each term. Tryouts for our interscholastic teams begin after classes tomorrow. Times and locations can be found in the *Daily Docket*. If you are not selected for a team, or have no interest, our intramural sports will begin on Wednesday. All students must enroll by the end of classes next Friday."

As Sally described where and when we needed to be for the rest of the evening, I examined the list behind her. I had never heard of some of the sports. Most of the others sounded unappealing. I was no athlete.

But I had been dancing for over a decade. While I doubted *dance* meant the tap class I had taken at home, it was the only sport on the list that sounded like something I might enjoy.

Chapter 17

WHEN THE MEETING FINALLY ENDED, I JOINED THE tide of students rushing into the aisle and lost Sarah by the time I exited the auditorium. When she finally emerged, she was talking to one of the boys from our orientation group. That guy she had met over the summer. What was his name again? Lovable something. Luke? Leo? Larry?

That was it! Loveable Larry. That name thing really worked.

Good thing, since my roommate didn't bother introducing us as we exited the Science Center. As soon as we got outside, Sarah pointed to the VAPAC.

"Did anyone want to grab refreshments?"

Larry made a face. "Not really. I think I'd rather wait for dinner."

I nodded. I was in no mood to socialize with a bunch of people I didn't know.

As Larry walked with us toward the dorms, he and Sarah compared Hartfield to their previous schools. Like my roommate, this was not Larry's first time attending boarding school.

"This place is definitely bigger than my last school."

Sarah nodded. "I know, right? I am *so* glad I came here this summer." She turned to me. "I don't know how you do it. It took me, like, two weeks to find the dining hall."

I shrugged. "I kind of just picture this place like a giant square. The VAPAC, MAC, dining hall, and Woodward are the points."

Larry nodded at me with a knowing smile. "That's not bad. Wish I had thought of that over the summer. I walked around with the map like an idiot."

Sarah giggled. "I remember that. But it was only for a couple of days."

Larry shook his head. "No. I only carried the printout for a couple of days. Then I realized I could use the map app on my phone to get from point A to point B. It was less embarrassing."

Sarah and I entered our dorm laughing. I was a little surprised that Larry followed us inside. Instead of going upstairs, Sarah sat on a couch in the common room. Larry settled onto a neighboring one, so I sat on the opposite side of my roommate's.

We spent some time talking about our homes. While Sarah lived maybe an hour south of Hartfield, Larry had grown up in Rhode Island. Over the summer, however, his father had changed jobs and his family had moved to Pennsylvania.

Eventually, our conversation turned to today's meetings. After we all decided none of us were interested in running for either student government, we discussed our sports requirement.

Larry turned to me. "What sport are you trying out for, Melinda?"

I shrugged. "I'm not really into sports. But I've been dancing for years, so I guess I'll try that. How about you?"

"My roommate and I are really into football, so we're both trying out. I'm pretty sure everyone who doesn't make varsity gets on JV." He looked at Sarah expectantly.

She smiled. "I played field hockey last year. It was a lot of fun, so I'm going to try out for that."

I had no idea what she was talking about. I had heard of ice hockey and we had played floor hockey in gym class in school. Was field hockey like one of those?

I didn't get to ask. Sarah changed the subject. "Hey. Did anyone else get freaked out when the college counselor introduced himself?"

Larry laughed. "I was expecting him to tell us we had to pick out our top choices for colleges during study hours tonight."

I shook my head. "I'm still wrapping my head around that fact that I'm here and not at my local high school. College? That's just too far away."

Sarah smiled. "I know, right? I mean, I'd like to do something with music, but I don't know what. And when I was little, I wanted to be a vet. I don't think I want to anymore, but what if I change my mind again?"

Larry leaned a little closer to her, an excited smile on his face. "Exactly. I mean, I think I want to play football in college, but I'm not sure what I want to study. I have a lot of interests."

They both turned to me. I bit my lip. "I have no idea. I mean, I'm not that good at anything. Last night, at dinner? I don't know about you guys, but at my table, everyone was talking about their talents and hobbies. One girl won a bunch of awards for piano. The guy next to him was recruited for the math team. Someone was great at football. And I was just sitting there thinking how there wasn't anything special about me."

Sarah sent me a sympathetic smile. "That's not true."

I shook my head. "I didn't mean it like that. I just mean, I don't *know* what I'm good at."

Larry nodded. "I felt like that last year. I think it's a boarding school thing. But, that's the best part of high school. You have all these opportunities to find yourself."

Sarah nodded. "Yeah. I mean, I never would have known I liked field hockey if I didn't learn about it at my old school."

I raised my eyebrows. "What *is* field hockey?"

She giggled. "See? It's kind of like ... hmm. I'm not sure how to explain it. You see, there's a ball like a big golf ball. And we have these flat sticks that we have to use to hit the ball into the goal."

I couldn't picture it. But I could probably look it up online. I gave a polite smile.

Larry glanced at his phone. "Hey. I'm getting hungry. You guys want to see if the picnic's ready yet?"

When Sarah and I both nodded, Larry led the way out of the dorm and back to the VAPAC. The lawn where we had made our giant knot at orientation looked a lot like the dining hall had last night. Two long tables, each covered with black tablecloths, held an extensive selection of food. Drink dispensers were at another station off to the side. However, unlike last night, students weren't in special dress, seated at tables. They were sitting in small groups all over the lawn.

And it wasn't just those of us who were new. The dining hall and snack bar were closed tonight, so every student from each form was here. It was a little overwhelming.

Sarah and I followed Larry to the shortest food line and soon had paper plates in our hands as we stared at our options. The burgers looked a little overcooked and dry, but I was willing to try one. Especially once I lathered it with cheese, onions, mustard, ketchup, and mayonnaise. After scooping some potato salad and chips onto my plate, I grabbed a brownie and cookie and searched for my roommate.

She was near the beverage table. I joined her, taking a bottle of water. She pointed to a group of students close to us.

"Larry went to sit with his roommate."

She didn't ask if we should join them. She must have assumed we would. As we approached the cluster, I recognized Awesome Andy from our orientation group, as well as two other boys whose names I had forgotten.

Larry helped by making introductions. "Hey. So, Sarah, Melinda? This is my roommate, Andy. That's his sister Andrea. She's in your dorm."

The girl made a face. "I told you, I prefer Dre."

Larry shook his head and pointed to the people beside Dre. "That's Xandra and Caroline. And Forrest and Leif are in the room next to us."

I nearly choked on my burger. "I'm sorry. I know this is probably extremely rude, but did anyone else catch that? Forest and Leaf? Sharing a room? That's funny. I'm sorry, but it is."

Leif smiled. "Yeah, I thought so, too. My parents named me after my great-grandfather. When I met Forrest yesterday, I just cracked up."

As we ate, I learned a lot about my new classmates. While Caroline, Forrest, and I had only ever attended public school, the others had all been in private school their whole lives, though only Larry and Sarah had been to boarding school. We discussed which sports everyone would try, and I was glad to see I wasn't the only person considering in an intramural. Caroline had no interest in a sport and was thinking of taking yoga or aerobics instead.

She was a flautist like me, while Sarah played the clarinet. As they discussed the musical ensembles at Hartfield, I realized they sounded like my school band and I would probably sign up next week as well.

Caroline was also interested in the choral groups, as were Forrest and Dre. Although I had participated in both band and chorus in middle school, I wasn't positive I wanted to sing here, so I kept quiet.

Unlike last night's dinner, we were free to come and go as we pleased. As we ate, more students arrived, but even more left. Soon, daylight was disappearing, and we decided it was time to change into our special dress.

When I had packed for Hartfield, I hadn't imagined needing so many dressy outfits. I stared at the limited selection in my closet. Didn't someone mention there was a shuttle to a nearby mall? I would definitely need to look into that.

For now, I would have to settle for what I had. My eyes landed on my black floral skirt. Of course! It was one of my favorites. It had large white flowers of different shapes and sizes overlapping each other. The bottom few inches was a black eyelet and a black ribbon wrapped around my waist a few times before dangling from my side.

And I had the perfect blouse to match it. Entirely black, an overlay covered the short-sleeved shirt that was fitted from the collar until just below my chest, where it flowed loosely. The lower half of the shirt had an embroidered flower pattern that matched my skirt perfectly.

Although I had been wearing them all day, my black flip-flops were dressy enough to go with this outfit. More importantly, however, they were more comfortable than the only formal shoes I had brought.

After changing, Sarah and I waited in the common room for the girls we had met at dinner. Somewhere on the way back, we had all agreed to walk to the VAPAC together. I sat on the couch, slipping off my shoes and tucking my legs under my skirt.

Even though I had slept well last night, I was tired. Resting my head against the back of the couch, I closed my eyes and considered everything I had done today. Meetings that lasted forever. So much walking.

Even though I had yet to attend any classes, I had accomplished more today than I had in an average week in my old school. Was every day going to be this grueling?

I hoped not.

Chapter 18

SARAH'S LOUD VOICE JARRED ME FROM MY MUSINGS. "Looks like we're ready to go!"

Opening my eyes, I glanced around. Had I fallen asleep? I was certainly drowsy, like something had awakened me from a nap. And there were a lot more girls in the room.

Our group was much larger than I had been expecting. Jade and Jessi had joined us, as well as two other girls from our floor and three more from Xandra's. I let everyone walk out of the dorm while I slipped my shoes onto my feet. I was the last one outside.

The girls had stopped to talk with a group of boys that had obviously been waiting for us. I recognized some of them from our orientation group, but others I had never met.

As we walked to the VAPAC, I saw more clusters of people heading in the same direction. Some knots were as large as ours. They were the ones coming from Woodward and Stanton. The upper formers seemed to prefer smaller groups.

When we entered the theater, Larry turned to the group. "So, where should we sit?"

Someone I didn't recognize frowned. "Didn't Mr. Birkenhead say to sit on the stage?"

Sarah nodded. "Yeah. But how do we *get* there?"

I bit my lip. At my old school, as well as the theater where I had my dance recitals, there was a door on the side of the auditorium that led to the backstage area. I turned to Sarah.

"I have an idea. Lemme check something. Don't, you know, leave without me."

I quickly ducked into the theater entrance. I was facing several rows of seats. But there was no way to the stage. There wasn't even a set of steps to get there from the front row.

With a sigh, I went to report my findings to my classmates. Halfway there, I spotted Mr. Birkenhead. Although the thought of approaching the man who was essentially my principal scared me, I didn't want to climb onto the stage in front of the entire school.

I bit my lip as I approached. "Um, Mr. Birkenhead?" My voice was so quiet, I wasn't sure he heard me.

But he must have. He turned to face me with a smile. "Hello."

"Hi. Uh, you, um, you told us we were supposed to, uh, sit on the stage tonight?"

Mr. Birkenhead nodded. "Yes. That's right."

"Um, the thing is? We, uh, don't know how to get there. Without, you know, climbing up from the theater."

Mr. Birkenhead's chuckle rang through the lobby. I could feel my cheeks warm. Was he laughing because we were lost?

"Climbing from the theater. That's a good one." He jerked his head toward the right side of the lobby, pointing over his shoulder. "Come on. I'll show you."

143

I turned to my classmates, quickly gesturing for them to join me before following Mr. Birkenhead. We passed a wide staircase leading upstairs. Just beyond the restrooms, the dean opened a door.

As he used his foot to lower the kickstand, he gestured down the hallway. "Follow this corridor. You'll see the stage entrance to your left."

I gave a weak smile. "Thanks."

I felt at home in this corridor. It reminded me of so many dance recitals. As we looked for the stage, I saw the dressing room to my right, then the greenroom. Across the hallway was the stage door. Someone had propped it open.

I stepped through it slowly. Even though I was still in the wings, I could see the theater. Students occupied many of the orchestra seats. I glanced up. The balcony was pretty packed, too.

But on the stage were dozens of rows of black chairs, all facing the podium on the opposite end. Those seats were empty. And I didn't want to be the first student to walk onto the stage in front of my entire school.

Thankfully, my friends were less scared. Larry walked to the second to last row of seats, sitting in the chair furthest upstage. Sarah sat beside him. Slowly, my group filled the row, as well as the row behind it. Uncertain where else to sit, I chose the seat in front of my roommate.

I watched students trickle into the theater. As much as I hated knowing everyone could see me, I enjoyed being able to watch all of them. I saw an upper former enter the room with her friend. Based on their outfits and how animatedly the two were talking, I tried to guess which form they were. They were both wearing makeup and barely looked around the theater before sitting. While they waited for the meeting, they turned to talk to the people near them. They had to be sixth formers. I had no clue if I was right, but it was a fun game.

I guessed the forms for a few other students before looking away. It surprised me to see the theater so crowded. The stage was full. I hadn't even realized I was peering around other third formers.

The headmaster walked to the podium and raised a hand. The room grew silent.

"Good evening." His voice boomed over the speakers throughout the auditorium. Any lingering whispers were silenced. "And welcome to the start of another school year. Let us begin by rising to sing the school song."

I wanted to groan with the rest of my classmates. But as I got to my feet, I realized no one was complaining. Was I the only person sick of this song?

The first few bars played over the speakers, and the entire theater erupted into song. I had never heard anything like it. When we had practiced in the dorm yesterday, our voices were loud. When we sang for our supper last night, there were more of us, but we were outside.

But tonight, the entire school was singing. Every student and teacher. I couldn't even hear the music over all the voices. As I sang, I felt the power of this song. For the first time, I understood why the deans had insisted we memorize the words.

I was still reveling in the song's power as we returned to our seats. I couldn't wait to hear the great pearls of wisdom from our headmaster. When I realized I was literally sitting on the edge of my seat, I forced myself to relax and scooch back.

Unfortunately, his speech was a short story about what he had done over his summer vacation, followed by a list of improvements to the school during the break. Houses I couldn't identify had been renovated. New library resources had been purchased. Parking lots had been repaved.

I had long lost interest when he stated the school's mission and vision for the upcoming year. I was sure he intended his speech to be inspiring, and I got the impression he was giving us suggestions for how to be successful. However, he was using so many big words and analogies I couldn't understand that I found it difficult to follow.

I closed my eyes, instantly feeling my earlier fatigue. Although I did not fall asleep, the headmaster's words felt more like background music than a speech.

Loud clapping broke my trance. I opened my eyes to see the headmaster walking away from the podium. Students around me were getting to their feet. At first, I thought it was a standing ovation. But I quickly realized everyone was exiting the auditorium.

I glanced at my phone. We had a little time before study hours. I followed Sarah and the rest of our group off the stage, nearly losing them in the mass of third formers in the corridor.

When we finally reached the courtyard, I saw students going in all directions. Some were entering the gallery side of the VAPAC. Others were heading toward the MAC. I even saw several groups walking up the hill to the language building. Hadn't someone mentioned there were more dorms beyond it?

I followed the flood of students returning to Woodward. I was too tired to take part in any conversations and didn't linger outside to talk to the boys, as many of my classmates did.

After changing into pajamas, I brushed my teeth and got ready for bed. Sarah and I returned to our room at the same time. She frowned.

"Are you going to bed already?"

I shrugged. "I just wanted to get comfortable."

"I hear that. I'm going to change. Don't go to bed, yet, okay? I want to show you something."

Nodding, I climbed onto my bed. Although I remembered what the college counselor had said about doing our schoolwork there, we hadn't had any classes. What exactly were we supposed to study tonight?

Sarah changed into her pajamas. When she picked up her laundry bag, I assumed she was placing her dirty clothes inside. I didn't expect her to dump the contents onto her bed.

I raised my eyebrows. "Uh, what are you doing?"

She smirked. "You'll see. You do it, too."

"Why?"

"Because what else are we going to do during study hours?"

I didn't see how dumping our clothes was anything like studying, but I followed her lead. It wasn't as if there was a lot in there. I had only been here for two days.

Sarah rummaged through her desk, pulling out a handful of markers and tossing them onto her bed. She climbed beside them, indicating I should join her.

"I got these at a dollar store in the mall near my old school. I wanted to do this last night. But you fell asleep before we could."

I frowned. "I'm sorry! I—"

Sarah waved a dismissive hand. "Eh, don't worry about it. I was exhausted, too. Besides, it's perfect for study hours."

147

When we had received the bags, the woman manning the booth had instructed us to write our name, dorm, and room number on the white strip. But it was large enough that Sarah and I had room to embellish the information with colorful flowers and artistic swirls. Following Sarah's lead, I even drew some confetti and butterflies.

It was the perfect way to study before my first night of school.

Chapter 19

SATURDAY MORNING, I WOKE ABOUT TEN MINUTES before my alarm. I rolled over, not quite ready to get out of bed. A few minutes wouldn't make me late for my classes.

I sat bolt upright. My classes. Where were they? During all of orientation, I had never given my schedule more than a cursory glance. Where was the last place I even had it?

Thursday. It felt like forever ago. My father had handed it to the person at the textbook distribution. Then what? Had the man not returned it?

No. He had. I had seen it when I unpacked my books. It was inside one of them. Had I touched it since?

I glanced at my desk. I couldn't see my schedule, but the books were arranged haphazardly. A large hardcover textbook was resting on a thick paperback. It was a wonder they hadn't fallen.

I had a few minutes before my alarm. It wouldn't hurt to organize the books. I frowned at them. The textbook on top and a thinner paperback workbook both said *physics*. I placed them upright against the back wall, spines facing me. Beside them, I placed the two softcover books that said *Latin*. My single geometry text went next, followed by the last four paperbacks.

My schedule was resting at the bottom of the pile. With an enormous sigh of relief, I collapsed into my chair and studied it. Without intending to, I had organized my books in the order I would have each subject. I closed my eyes, trying to imagine going from one class to another.

Trinity had said she had pointed out each of the academic buildings. And I knew the day started at eight. But how long was each class period? How much time did I have to get from one building to another? And hadn't Sally said something about a modified schedule today?

I leafed through the black orientation folder, finding the daily class times listed on a page in the back. They were normally fifty minutes long, but on Saturdays and Wednesdays, they were only half an hour, with a form meeting between fourth and fifth period. I had ten minutes to get from one class to another. Would that be enough?

My alarm rang, causing me to jump, even though it wasn't very loud. After silencing it, I rushed to get a shower before the rest of my floor.

Getting dressed was a challenge. I had to change three times before I found an outfit that matched the dress code. It was going to take a while to adjust to not wearing jeans and a T-shirt every day.

While Sarah was in the shower, I stared at my desk. Was I supposed to carry all those books to class? I hadn't forgotten how heavy they were. Frowning, I considered my options. I had a few free periods. I could probably carry a few and return to the dorm to swap my books then.

But was that really necessary? It was the first day of school. I doubted I would need them today. Better to bring a single notebook and mark which books each class required. When I pulled my notebook from the drawer, I caught sight of the assignment pad my mother had bought with the rest of my school supplies. With a sigh, I grabbed that as well. Not that I expected my teachers to assign anything today. But they might ask us to buy something and I wanted to be able to write it down.

Tossing the two notebooks into my backpack, I headed to the dining hall. I would have loved to wait for my roommate, but I worried she would make me too late. Half an hour didn't feel like a lot of time to eat and get across campus to the VAPAC loft. Maybe I could eat as I walked.

I used the side entrance to the dining hall, heading straight to the servery. After placing a raisin bagel in the toaster, I went back to the dining hall.

It wasn't very crowded, although there were definitely more people than yesterday. I walked to the nearest table and grabbed a handful of napkins from the dispenser. When my toast was done, I wrapped it in a napkin and took it to the toppings bar, slathering a thick layer of cream cheese onto it.

I wasn't sure if we were allowed to take food from the dining hall, so I wrapped the bagel in the napkin and held it close as I made my way through the senior section. No one stopped me, however, and as soon as I cleared the front steps, I bit into my breakfast. By the time I reached the intersection, I was wishing I had thought to bring a drink. If this was going to be a regular thing, I would have to start carrying my water bottle around with me.

I finished my bagel before reaching the VAPAC. After a quick sip from the water fountain, I glanced at the clock above it. I still had a bit of time before class. As eager as I was to explore the loft, I didn't want to sit up there all by myself, so I settled onto a couch for a few minutes.

From my perch, I could see through the glass windows into the courtyard. A boy and girl were approaching, using the same path I had from the dining hall. Had they been behind me the entire way?

They were talking animatedly and, as soon as they entered, their voices echoed in the vast gallery. It sounded as if they were discussing a musical, since I heard things like *audition* and *sing*. But, they were using many big words I didn't understand, so I couldn't be sure.

Neither of them seemed to notice me as they walked up to the loft. I took that as my cue that I could go upstairs. Grabbing my bag from the floor, I followed them.

The staircase was narrow and steep. It was intimidating enough for me to hold the rail like a toddler. But I didn't mind. At the top, I was rewarded with a view of the loft that I had wanted to see since I first arrived at Hartfield.

It was larger than I had expected. It had never occurred to me that it would be the same size as the gallery, even though its floor was the ceiling for the lower level.

To my left, more or less directly above the partition near the water fountain, was a glass wall. I could see desks and easels on the other side, though no people.

The front of the loft, facing the courtyard, was one long table with a bunch of stools beneath it. The boy and girl were sitting on two, in a conversation so intense that they had yet to notice me.

On the other side of the loft was a similar table, though no one would dare sit there because of all the junk. There were no other words to describe what I was seeing. An old tricycle. A small table piled with unidentifiable knickknacks. A bowl filled with what I hoped was plastic fruit, not anything fresh.

That side of the room was a lot darker than where I was standing. When I looked up, I realized there was another loft overlooking this one. It was about half as large and there were no stairs.

"You can sit down, you know."

I turned to the wry voice. The boy and girl had stopped talking and were watching me with humorous expressions.

The girl rolled her eyes. "We don't bite. Well, I don't. Luke might."

Biting my lip, I hurried to a stool near the boy, who was closer to me, though I kept a seat between me and him.

"Oh, uh, sorry." I placed my bag on the floor under the table before turning slightly to face my new classmates.

The boy shook his head. "Don't mind her. She can be a real pain before noon."

The boy's tone was much pleasanter than the girl's had been. He smiled. "I'm Luke. That's my sister Lizzie."

The girl scowled at her brother before looking at me. "It's Liz."

I gave a small wave. "Melinda."

Luke sent me a warm smile. "Are you new this year?"

I nodded. "Third form."

Luke gestured to himself and his sister a few times. "We're fourth form. Mr. Rockwell is a great art teacher. You'll like him a lot. He really loves the subject and gets very excited when talking about it. Plus, he brings Ruby to almost every class and she's so sweet."

"Ruby?"

Liz rolled her eyes. "His pug?"

"Really? He brings his dog to class?"

Liz shrugged. "A lot of teachers do. Ruby's pretty good. She doesn't get in the way when we're sketching. But you can't draw her."

"Why not?" I instantly envisioned a dog who bit anyone holding a pencil.

Luke smiled. "Because she's so hyper. She won't even sit long enough for you to pet her. As soon as you try to sketch her, she moves out of the way."

As other students entered the loft, Luke greeted them. Liz, meanwhile, folded her arms on the table and buried her head, as if she were trying to take a nap before class started. Based on the snippets of conversation I overhead, several of the students had been in art class together previously.

At exactly eight o'clock, a tall man walked into the loft from the glass room. He had dark skin and white hair and had to be at least six and a half feet tall. But I was more impressed by his outfit. Except for gym class, my teachers had always worn what my mother called *business casual*. But not this man. His dark jeans and light shirt contained paint splatters in so many colors, it was difficult to determine what they originally may have looked like.

Beside him trotted a dog that could not have weighed ten pounds. Ruby could have easily fit in Mr. Rockwell's hand, though she ran so many circles around the loft, I wasn't sure he could catch her if he wanted to hold her.

Mr. Rockwell grabbed a stool from the back of the room and placed it in the middle of the loft, settling on it with a smile.

"Good morning. My name is Donald Rockwell, and this is drawing class. I am originally from Newport News, Virginia, and I have been teaching here for twenty years. I know some of you, but why don't we just go around the room and introduce ourselves. Tell us your name, where you're from, and what year you are."

Mr. Rockwell pointed to the boy sitting beside Liz at the end of the long table. By the time the person closest to the stairs introduced himself, I realized I was the only third former. Was I in the wrong class? I wasn't an artist. I had trouble drawing stick people.

After the introductions, Mr. Rockwell walked to the table in the back of the room and grabbed a small pile of boxes, which he passed to each of us. I had seen oil crayons like these before. We had used them in my middle school. Except, this was a brand new box. The crayons weren't smushed and broken. He also had enough for each of us to get our own box. I had always had to share supplies at my old school.

Mr. Rockwell then distributed a large sketchbook to each of us. The book was nearly as long as my arm. How was I supposed to carry this thing?

Apparently, in the large paper suitcase Mr. Rockwell called a *portfolio*. It was the same brown as the sketchbook, but it had a string to fasten the flap and a black handle to carry it. While it was large enough to hold our new supplies, it was bulky. Was I expected to carry this around campus all day? Every day?

Mr. Rockwell spent the rest of the class period describing what we would learn during the term. I didn't understand him well enough to follow what he was saying. Until I heard the word *homework*. Surely, he didn't mean for tonight, but I tried to pay closer attention anyway.

"I look forward to seeing your drawings on Monday." With a small wave, he stood.

So did my classmates. Mr. Rockwell had dismissed us. But what was that part about the homework? What were we supposed to be drawing?

I stayed in my seat as my classmates made their way out of the loft. Some tried to pet Ruby, but she dashed away before they could reach her. As she followed students down the spiral stairs, I made my way to Mr. Rockwell.

Standing beside him, I felt so tiny. It took a lot of effort to make sure my voice didn't squeak.

"Um, Mr., uh, Rockwell?"

He turned to me. "Yes, Melinda, right?"

"Yeah. I mean, well, I just had a quick question. I heard you say something about homework, but I sort of missed what the actual assignment was. I know we're drawing something, but, well, what are we drawing?"

Mr. Rockwell sent me a warm smile. "That's the assignment. I want you to draw me something. Anything you would like. It can be a still life or it can come from your imagination. You can use pencil or your new oil crayons. It's entirely up to you."

"Oh. Okay. Well, thanks." Grabbing my backpack and portfolio, I headed downstairs.

I could draw whatever I wanted. Did that include stick figures?

Chapter 20

IT WAS STILL PASSING TIME, BUT SECOND PERIOD would be starting soon. Not that I was concerned. I didn't have a class and my following one wasn't far away. But, though I knew it was in the Science Center, I didn't know *where* it was. Maybe I could use my free period to find my next classroom.

I entered the door opposite the one I had used every time we had visited this building yesterday. On my right was a small corridor. With a shrug, I ventured down it. The sign beside the closest door read 106. According to my schedule, I was in 104. That had to be nearby, right?

I kept walking. There were two more classrooms, one on my left and one at the end of the hall. The closer one was room 104, but the door was closed and the lights were off. I had no desire to sit in an empty classroom for half an hour.

Instead, I would explore the building. So far, I had only been to Baker Auditorium. I continued along the horseshoe. Near the other set of doors was a wide staircase. I followed it to the second story, finding myself at the entrance. Through the glass doors, I could see the bridge over the pond.

There were more classrooms on this level, as well as what might have been a teacher's lounge. As I continued along the curve, I found a few corridors. The first held classrooms. A spiral staircase was down the second. At the end of the last hallway, I found the restrooms.

Directly opposite the main entrance was another exit, beyond which I could see the language building. I continued along the horseshoe, assuming I would find more classrooms. But there was a window in the wall beside the exit that made me curious. I had seen it almost immediately, but I couldn't see through it until I was standing beside it.

The window was round, about the size of my torso, although high enough that I could only just see in from where I was standing. The room on the other side didn't look into a classroom. Instead of desks, there were four oversized black chairs surrounding a small coffee table. Tucked into the back were some couches and a long counter that ran the length of a bank of windows looking outside.

I felt like I was peeking into a fishbowl. And I really wanted to go sit inside. Those chairs looked so comfy. And I would be able to put down the portfolio that was growing heavy in my hand.

But was I allowed in there? Or was it another teacher's lounge? How was anyone supposed to get in? I didn't see any doors.

"Are you alright?"

I turned to the man who had broken my trance. He was tall and lanky, with brown hair and glasses. And he was staring at me expectantly.

I nodded. "Yeah. I, uh, I was just, um, looking around." I couldn't explain why, but I felt like he had caught me doing something wrong.

The man smiled. "That's fine. Are you a new student? You look a little lost."

When I nodded, the man gestured to the room. "A lot of students like to spend their free periods in the lounge here. The lights will turn on when you enter."

"Thanks." I avoided the man's gaze. I still didn't know *how* to enter the room, but I was too embarrassed to ask.

With a nod, the man turned and headed down the spiral staircase. I waited until he had disappeared before continuing along the horseshoe. The corridor was much like the one downstairs where my classroom was. But I didn't see an entrance to the lounge.

When I reached the end of the corridor, I turned around and gasped. I had missed a door. And not just any door. It was the entrance to the fishbowl lounge!

I was almost giddy as I settled into one of the chairs. There was still some time before class and I wanted to copy my schedule into the front cover of my assignment pad. I had learned in middle school that writing it down helped me memorize it faster.

I dug through my bag for the set of colored pens I had bought this summer. They matched my binders. As I copied my schedule, I selected a different color for each subject.

Art was first. I used the black pen, noticing I did not have class on Wednesday. It surprised me to see a column for Saturday as well. My old assignment books never had one.

As I entered physics in purple, Latin in pink, geometry in green, and English in blue, I noticed each class only met five times a week. That must have been what Sally meant when she said there were no teacher free days today. I was pretty sure the free day was the day we didn't have class.

When I finished copying my schedule, I turned to today's date and entered my art assignment. Did I have time to start it now?

I glanced through the round window. People were flooding the hallways. They were entering and exiting the science center. Going in and out of classrooms on this floor. Checking the outside window, I could see people walking to and from the language building and VAPAC.

I gathered my things and took the smaller staircase downstairs. I was a little surprised to see it spiraled around a giant pendulum. The bulb at the bottom was easily as tall as my waist and it was oscillating slowly. It was mesmerizing, and I probably could have stared at it for hours.

But, I didn't want to be late for physics. When I entered the classroom, I stood just inside the door while I tried to decide where to sit. Instead of desks, the room had sixteen small tables, each with two chairs behind it. All but two were occupied. I chose the empty desk near the door, tucking my portfolio between my legs and the table's. After removing my notebook and assignment pad, I tucked my bag beneath my chair and turned to the front of the room.

The teacher was standing behind a large black lab bench, similar to the ones where we had done our experiments in middle school. He was writing on the board, but I recognized his shirt. He was the man who had introduced me to the fishbowl lounge.

A few more students entered the room before the teacher closed the door. We sat in silence as he returned to the lab bench and glanced at the tablet before him. Finally, he looked up with a smile.

"Good morning. My name is Ted Wilson. You may call me Mr. Wilson. This is my third year teaching physics here at Hartfield. I am originally from Minnesota. I'm going to read my roster. When I call your name, please raise your hand and tell me your dorm."

His introductory speech was lifeless and boring. Was every class going to be like this? How would I learn anything if I was struggling to stay awake?

Mr. Wilson called a few names. The first person lived in Stanton. The next one was in Woodward. But then, another girl was in Library and a boy lived in Hall. Weren't all third formers supposed to be in Woodward or Stanton?

"Melinda Luzzelli?"

I was so lost in my thoughts, I nearly missed my own name. I quickly raised my hand. "Uh, Woodward."

Mr. Wilson nodded and continued the roll call. When he was done, he strolled through the room twice, passing out a different handout each time. The first one described the course and Mr. Wilson read it aloud. Why had he bothered to give us a copy? Maybe in case I fell asleep listening to him?

"Now, if you look at the other handout, this is your syllabus for the term."

What was a *syllabus*? I quickly scribbled the word in the notes section at the bottom of my assignment pad. I would look it up after class.

"As you can see, I have listed each day we will be meeting and the topic we will be discussing. If you look at today's date, you will see today's topic is *Course Overview*. The assignment listed in the *Assignment* column is due next class."

Twenty pages. I had to read the first twenty pages of my textbook over the weekend. With a groan, I entered the assignment in my pad beneath my art homework. After tucking the handouts in the back, I returned my attention to the front of the room.

Mr. Wilson was writing on the board. Was I supposed to be copying it? I glanced around. Most of my classmates were taking notes.

I opened my own notebook and copied the information. Mr. Wilson was writing his biography. His name. The room number of his office. His dorm. The phone numbers for both his office and home extensions. His office hours. The times he was on duty.

While I was still copying the information, Mr. Wilson turned to face us. "Please feel free to visit me during my office hours. You may also visit when I am on duty, but please let your advisor know where you will be during study hours."

I was confused. Did he mean he wanted us to visit him *at his home* during study hours? Why would we do that?

"Oh, it looks like we are out of time. Have a great weekend and I'll see you all on Monday."

I quickly finished copying the rest of the information on the board. Tossing my notebook and assignment pad into my backpack, I grabbed my portfolio and hurried out of the classroom before Mr. Wilson could assign us even more work for the weekend.

I had another free period before our form meeting. I wanted to return to the fishbowl lounge and wallow about getting homework on the first day of school. But I figured a better use of my time would be to find my Latin class.

At the top of the staircase, I turned to the exit that would take me to the language building. And nearly crashed into Sarah, who was entering the Science Center. She sent me a warm smile.

"Hey, Roomie! How's your morning going?"

"Ugh. Who gives homework on the first day?"

"I know, right? Where you heading?"

I shrugged. "I'm free. I wanted to find my Latin class."

"I'm free, too. I'll go with you. I was just there. That place is such a maze."

I followed Sarah up the hill. As we approached, I realized the place was basically three smaller buildings arranged in a triangle that pointed downhill. There was a small courtyard between the three sections. Sarah led me down the concrete steps, pointing to a door on the lower left side of the building.

"So, I was just in Room 3. Why don't we start there and see if we can find, what is it?"

"Room 12. Sounds good to me."

I followed her into the building and found myself in a circular room with five doors and a stairwell. Three of them contained numbers almost as large as me. One had a letter instead. The last door was the one we had just entered.

Sarah shook her head. "Okay. So, no Room 12. Should we try upstairs?"

I shrugged. "Might as well."

Upstairs was nearly identical to downstairs. There was a door to outside. There were Rooms B, C, and D. There was also a hallway to connect this wing to the next one. Sarah and I followed it, finding Room 4, another staircase, and a new corridor.

Sarah frowned. "Maybe your class is downstairs?"

I was pretty sure it was down the hall, but I followed my roommate. The door at the bottom of the stairs led to a computer lab. Along one side of the room was a large librarian's desk, behind which sat a woman and several file cabinets. On the opposite side, I could see the courtyard through the windows and glass door. The rest of the room was divided into cubicles, each with a laptop and heavy-duty headphones.

I was glad we had taken the time to explore the building. How many of my classmates were going to be late because they got lost in this maze?

Sarah and I backtracked up the stairs and continued to the right wing of the building. There, we found Rooms 9 through 12. Feeling victorious, I led the way outside and back down the hill to the fishbowl lounge.

We had the room to ourselves. Sinking into a chair with a groan, I nodded to my roommate across from me.

"So. How have your classes been?"

Sarah shrugged. "My music class sounds like it's going to be a lot of fun. German, not so much. My teacher spent half the class speaking in German before she realized none of us could understand her. How about you? And what is that thing?"

I told her about my art class, showing her my sketch pad and crayons. Rolling my eyes, I held up my portfolio as I returned its contents. "I have the pleasure of carrying this thing around with me all day."

Sarah frowned. "Maybe you can stop by the dorm between classes."

I shrugged. "Maybe. I have no more free periods today, though."

"Yeah. Me either. I've got physics, math, then English."

"I have Latin, math, and English."

"Hey. Wouldn't it be cool if we had the same classes?"

I shook my head as I pulled my schedule from my bag. "How did we not think to do this before?"

"I know, right? Frankly, orientation was just so much, you know? I didn't even look at my schedule until this morning."

I nodded, passing my paper to Sarah. "Yeah, me neither. So, what's the verdict? Do we have the same classes?"

She took a moment to compare the two schedules. "Hey, we do!" She returned the paper to me. "That's so cool. Okay. So, I'll wait for you in the hallway just outside this room and we can go to math together."

I smiled. "Sounds good to me."

Chapter 21

I HAD LOST TRACK OF HOW MANY MEETINGS I HAD attended during orientation. Why did we need yet another form meeting? What hadn't the deans told us yet?

After Sally welcomed us to our first day of classes, she went over the schedule for the rest of the weekend. Then Mr. Birkenhead reminded us of the sports requirements and encouraged us to consider running for student government. Sally had some more comments about our class schedules and textbooks. None of this information was new, although I did scribble a few unfamiliar words into my assignment pad to look up later.

Finally, the meeting ended, and Sally dismissed us to our fifth periods. I joined the small group of students heading up the hill. Unlike many of my classmates, I found my way effortlessly. I even gave a few people directions before entering Room 12.

I was the first one there. Although the lobby had been circular, this room was rectangular. How was that possible?

It was also the first classroom I had seen today with the same desks I had used in middle school. The plastic writing surface was attached to the chair with two metal bars. While about a dozen of them were facing the whiteboard at the front of the room, two were under the board pointed toward the classroom.

I sat with my back against the windows, at a desk that allowed me to watch the students trudging up the hill. The school architects must have been addicted to glass. There were so many windows at Hartfield. But, now that I considered it, none of my teachers had seemed to need a light switch today.

I was so busy staring outside, I barely noticed my classmates entering the room. A few minutes later, the teacher at my table the other night followed them, placing a stack of papers on one of the desks under the whiteboard before sitting at the other one. He was so tall, I wasn't sure how he expected to fit, but somehow, he managed, stretching his long legs in front of him.

"Good morning. Welcome to first-year Latin. Why don't we get to know each other a little better? I live in Katzmann house with my wife and our two little girls, as well as eight sixth-form girls. What about all of you? Tell me a little about yourselves. Name, form, and why you decided to take Latin."

The door opened, and a boy popped his head into the room.

"Is this Spanish?"

Mr. Henderson stood, shaking his head as he walked to the door. "No."

The boy frowned. "I'm trying to find my Spanish class. It's in Room 4. Do you know where that is?"

Mr. Henderson pointed down the corridor. "Baja que el vestíbulo y usted lo encontrarán."

When the boy gave him a puzzled look, my teacher repeated himself, a little slower this time. While my class was giggling, the boy continued to stare blankly.

Mr. Henderson shook his head. "Now I see why you need to find your classroom. Go down the hallway and you should see it."

Mr. Henderson closed the door and returned to his seat. "He said he was looking for Spanish. I assumed he was fluent. Oh well. Where were we? Oh, yes. You were going to introduce yourselves. Why don't you go first?"

The girl closest to the door shrugged. "My name is Lara. I'm a sixth former. And I thought taking Latin would help me with the SATs."

The boy beside her looked a little surprised that we were all staring at him. "Oh. Uh, I'm Roman. I'm in third form. And I'm taking Latin because my mother is making me."

Even though his face was turning red, none of us laughed. Wasn't I taking this class for more or less the same reason?

Except, when it was my turn, I opted for a slightly altered version of the truth. "Hi. I'm Melinda. Third form. And I took Italian in middle school. Since that's not an option here, I figured Latin would be the next closest language."

I tuned out the rest of my classmates' introductions. I wasn't going to remember anyone, anyway.

After everyone had shared, Mr. Henderson explained his goals and expectations for the year before passing out a syllabus. I glanced at it. We had to read the first story in our textbook and answer the questions that followed. Even though

Mr. Henderson assured us the assignment was short and straightforward, I couldn't help feeling like it was too much for the first day of school.

Mr. Henderson dismissed us a few minutes early, and I went directly to the Science Center. By the time I reached the main entrance, classes in this building were letting out. A moment later, Sarah came up the stairs.

We compared our classes as we crossed the campus to the math building. Although Sarah's teacher wasn't Mr. Wilson, it sounded like her class had gone about the same as mine.

Our math class was on the second floor of the building. The tables were arranged in a U to face the whiteboard. Students occupied most of the seats, but Sarah and I managed to find two beside each other. Sure, we were near the front of the room, but at least we could sit together.

Our teacher was standing beside his desk in the front of the room. As I settled into my seat, I couldn't help thinking he looked like a stereotypical math nerd. His khaki pants were pressed and pleated. His button-down shirt was crisp and white. His horn-rimmed glasses were thick. But all of that paled to his pocket protector. I had never seen anyone wear one in real life, only on television. Of course, he needed it, because his shirt pocket was full of pens.

When he spoke, his voice was so quiet, I wasn't sure how the students in the back of the room could hear him. "Hello. My name is Mr. Davidson, and this is honors geometry. I'm going to take a quick roll call, just to be sure everyone is where they are supposed to be."

Unlike my other teachers, Mr. Davidson did not ask us to introduce ourselves. After determining he had the correct students, he held up a textbook.

"This is the book we are using this year. Please make sure your cover matches this one." He returned the text to the desk and picked up a stack of papers. "As you will see, this is your syllabus for the term. Tonight's assignment is at the top."

I glanced at it as he passed the papers around the room. We had to read a few pages and complete all the problems at the end of the section. Even though math had been easy for me since the fifth grade, I was not looking forward to doing the work. It was just one more thing to do this weekend.

As I copied the assignment into my pad, Mr. Davidson reviewed a few basic concepts on the board. I didn't bother writing them into my notebook, since I could do them in my sleep.

After class, Sarah and I walked to the Humanities building together. I followed my roommate into the side entrance and down a hallway, stopping abruptly when we entered a large room. Since our first day, I had noticed a huge round bank of windows jutting out of the middle of the building, but I hadn't thought much about it. Somehow, it never occurred to me it might be part of a larger space.

The room was round with windows taller than me, though the ceiling extended much higher. Several couches were arranged around a large coffee table, while more lined both walls. The doorway to my left looked like it might be the main entrance, although glancing out the window, I only saw more dorms. If I had designed this place, I would have turned the building to face the driveway and field on the other side.

I was in love with this room. I could curl up with a book on one of those couches and read here forever. Even though my grandmother's entire house could probably fit in this enormous room, I felt completely at home here.

"Melinda? You okay?"

I glanced up. Sarah had crossed the room and was waiting for me in the opposite hallway. I looked around one last time as I joined her. "It's so big."

"It's called the *Rotunda*. Because it's a round room. But, *come on*." She grabbed my hand and pulled me down the hallway. "We can look at it after class. If you dawdle, we'll be late."

There was a stairwell on our right, near the end of the corridor. The trek to the fourth floor was harder than I had expected. When we emerged, I was surprised at how small the area was. There were only two classrooms and an office on this floor.

Our room was right next to the stairwell. I followed my roommate inside. Tables had been arranged in a square with several chairs on each side. Sarah slid into a seat close to the door and I sat beside her. A moment later, our teacher entered the room, sitting around the corner from me.

Although he was bald, he looked a lot younger than most of my other teachers today. He glanced around the room with a smile.

"Good morning. Actually—" He glanced at his watch. "I should say *good afternoon*, shouldn't I?"

We all gave a polite laugh before he continued.

"I'm Mr. Johnson, and I'd like to learn all your names. I have a list here."

He held up his tablet before swiping and reading the first name. After going through the entire list, he handed me a stack of papers. I took one before passing it to Sarah.

Even as our teacher explained, I knew what this was. Another syllabus with more assignments. Mr. Johnson pointed at the door.

"As you can see at the top of the page, my office is here on the fourth floor, just across the hall. My office hours are listed there, as well as both my office and home extensions. Did everyone get a syllabus?"

When we all nodded, he held up a paperback. "You probably received three books for this class. The first is this anthology of Greek myths. Although we will not be reading all of them, I encourage you to read the rest in your free time. The more myths you know, the better you will understand *The Odyssey* when we get to it later in the term."

Mr. Johnson put down the book and held up another, even smaller one. "This is your vocabulary book. Every Friday, we will begin the class with a quick quiz. We will then read from your journals."

Mr. Johnson held up a marble composition notebook. "You should all purchase a book similar to this one. They are available at the school store, but you can buy them online or wherever. These are to be your writing journals."

Mr. Johnson spoke for a while about what we were to write in these books, emphasizing that he would be reading all our entries. While we only needed to share one with the class each Friday, we were required to write at least three every week.

As I copied tonight's assignment into my pad, I wanted to cry. I hadn't expected any of my teachers to give us homework tonight. Instead, all of them had, and it all sounded hard.

As I followed my roommate out of the classroom, I felt a sense of dread. Would the workload get harder as the year went on? Would I be able to keep up?

Did I even want to? Maybe, if I didn't do the homework, I would be able to go back home.

But was that really what I wanted anymore?

Chapter 22

NOW THAT CLASSES WERE FINALLY OVER, I COULDN'T wait to return to my room. I was exhausted. And I was sick of lugging my portfolio all over campus. No one else had one. I felt ridiculous.

But Sarah insisted I join her for lunch. So instead of returning to Woodward, we turned right out of Humanities and ventured to the dining hall.

With every other student in the school. I had never seen the building so busy. Although each table held eight chairs, there were more than twice that many students at some of the tables. I didn't want to wait for food, so I made myself a quick peanut butter and jelly sandwich, managing somehow not to drop my portfolio as I carried it and my tray to a table.

Sarah was sitting with a bunch of girls from our dorm. I could recognize them by sight, even though I didn't know anyone's name. While everyone compared their days, I zoned out. My sole focus was finishing my lunch and returning to my room. Possibly staying there forever.

But the girls seemed to be obsessed with the athletic center.

"I heard there's a jogging track on the second floor that overlooks the basketball courts."

"I heard they have a bunch of cardio machines."

"Well, I want to see the squash courts. Didn't the headmaster say they were renovated this summer?"

I didn't have the energy to ask what a vegetable had to do with sports. I just wanted to take a nap.

The girls were so eager to go exercise, they didn't linger in the dining hall. I followed them back to the dorm. While Sarah changed into athletic wear, I threw my backpack on my desk chair and my art portfolio on the floor. Kicking off my shoes, I plopped onto the bed. But I wanted my phone. Without moving from my perch, I reached into my bag and dug it out. It was dead.

Of course it was. I could never remember to charge the thing. Where had I left that charger?

I tried to recall the last time I had seen it. Hadn't I plugged it into the wall when I moved in? I glanced in the spot between my bed and the window. The cord was on the floor. It took a little effort, but I managed to grab it without getting off the bed. As I plugged in the phone, Sarah frowned at me.

"You sure you don't want to come with us?"

I nodded. "Positive."

"Okay. Well, I'll catch up with you later."

I gave her a small wave to let her know I didn't mind being alone, then returned my attention to my phone. It had just enough battery to turn on. Almost as soon as I did, I received a video chat request. With a sigh, I accepted the call.

Brittany's and Casey's faces both filled my screen. Brittany rolled her eyes. "Finally."

Casey shook her head. "Where have you *been*?"

I shrugged. "I had class this morning."

Both girls' eyes went wide. "On Saturday?"

"Yup. Today was our first day of classes."

Brittany made a disgusted face. "So, how is it there? Other than the school on the weekend thing."

"I am so tired. So much walking. So many buildings. So many new people. So much homework."

Casey groaned. "Homework? On the first day of school? Eww."

"How about you guys? How're things at home?"

Brittany's face lit up. "I think J is going to ask me out?"

I raised my eyebrows. "Who's Jay? And what happened to Greg?"

Casey rolled her eyes. "Don't you read your texts? They broke up on Thursday."

Brittany nodded. "He was always complaining I'm a big flirt because he's in bio with me and J, but then he stayed after on Thursday to work on something for auto class and Meg F saw him in the café making out with Paige Connors."

"So Meg texted Trish, who called Amber, who texted me. And I went to see Brittany at Drama club."

"Which was totally lame, so I walked out of the meeting and marched to the café and broke up with Greg right there. But that's fine because I think J's going to ask me out."

I held up a hand to interrupt my friends. "Wait. Who's this J guy?"

Casey rolled her eyes again. "Jacob Roberts? He goes by J now. You know. Just the letter?"

Brittany smiled. "He sits in front of me in bio and he keeps turning around in class to ask me questions. He's so cute. He pretends he doesn't know what's going on."

That was because he probably didn't. Jacob Roberts was an annoying jock who never knew what was going on. When we were studying Europe last year, he asked how Romania could be the capital of Italy if it was so far away. And he had been dead serious. How could Brittany be crazy about him?

I didn't get to ask. Casey squealed. "I just got a text from Francesca. Sue told her that Kevin said J is going to ask you out."

I raised my eyebrows. "Since when are Kevin and J friends? Or Sue and Francesca, for that matter?"

Brittany pursed her lips, speaking as if explaining something to Casey's little sister for the tenth time in a row. "Francesca and Sue are both cheerleaders. Kevin and J are both on the football team. Sue and Kevin are together."

Casey nodded. "How cute is that? SK and KS. Oh! I just got a great idea. Why don't I call Fitz and see if he wants to go to the movies tonight? He can ask J, and maybe J will ask you out!"

I was so confused. "Wait? Who's Fitz? I thought you were with Nick."

"Nick felt the soccer team was more important than me, so I dumped him in study hall on Wednesday. Dan Fitzpatrick was there, and he asked me out. So, what do you think?"

I thought Casey was asking my opinion of her new boyfriend. But Brittany responded before I could.

"Yeah. I'll go ask my mom if she can drive us."

I bit my lip. "Oh, hey. My phone is dying. I'll talk to you guys later."

They didn't even wave goodbye as I ended the call.

I felt guilty about lying to my two best friends, but I didn't want to listen to them plan a trip to the movies when I couldn't join them. I had already felt like a third wheel in the conversation. I had only been gone a few days, but so much had already changed at home.

Maybe talking to my parents would make me feel better. I hadn't spoken to either of them since they left me here Thursday. Maybe they missed me and had decided to take me home. I should have known better.

"Hi, Baby Girl. How are you?"

I shrugged, not that my mother could see me. "Fine, I guess."

"How were your classes today?"

"I have homework. On the first day of school."

My mother sighed. "We knew Hartfield would be different that what you were used to."

I scoffed. Maybe she knew, but I hadn't expected it.

"What about your teachers? Are they nice?"

"I guess. Most of them gave us their entire biography. I mean, why do I need to know when they're in their office or where they live? It's like they want us to stalk them."

My mother sighed again, and I had a feeling I was trying her patience. "Were you able to find your classes okay?"

"Yeah."

"And what about your classmates? Are you making friends?"

I considered all the people I had met the past few days. "I guess. Sarah and I are getting along okay. She's meeting a lot of people and I'm tagging along."

"I know this is hard. But I think if you give it a chance, you'll find you like it there."

My mother spent a few more minutes trying to convince me why sending me to Hartfield was the right decision. When she finally ended the call, I tossed my phone on my desk.

I didn't care what she said. I still wasn't convinced I belonged here.

Lying on my bed, I closed my eyes as I considered my day. Never in my life had I been so tired after the first day of school. Was it all the walking? Was it meeting so many new people? Was it all the homework?

I sighed. I probably should start some of that work. But what should I do first? Maybe I could write one of those journal entries for English. Talk about how unfair it was to have homework on the first day of school.

I DIDN'T KNOW I HAD FALLEN ASLEEP UNTIL I HEARD Sarah's whispered voice.

Sitting up, I rubbed my eyes and tried not to eavesdrop on my roommate's conversation.

"Oh, Mom. I better go . . . I love you, too . . . Bye." Sarah turned to me as she ended her call. "Sorry. I didn't mean to wake you."

I yawned and stretched. "No, it's fine. What time is it?"

Sarah smiled. "Dinnertime."

I had slept away my entire afternoon. But I felt a lot better than I had all day. My nap had definitely improved my mood.

Since the dining hall wasn't as crowded as it had been during lunch, I took my time exploring my options in the servery. After touring it twice, I opted for a sloppy joe sandwich.

I was scooping a little extra meat onto my roll when a boy from my orientation group joined me. I recognized him. He had been hanging around a lot. What was his name? Wacky something, right? Walter! Wacky Walter.

He must have recognized me as well. He smiled as he set his tray beside mine. "Ooh. That looks good. I think I'll try one."

I passed him the spoon with raised eyebrows. "Um, where are you going to put it?"

There was no room on his tray. He had already filled it with a bowl of soup, a small salad, and a grilled cheese. Frowning, he looked between our two trays a few times.

"Do you think maybe you can carry something for me?"

I shrugged. "I guess so."

"Thanks." Smiling, he moved his salad and sandwich to my tray before grabbing a plate from the stack beside the sloppy joe bar. I didn't wait for him. If he was hungry enough, he could come find me and the rest of his food.

After grabbing some water from the beverage island, I went in search of my roommate. She was sitting in the larger section of the dining hall, at the same table where we had eaten lunch. I recognized a few of the girls with her. They were from our dorm. They may have even been the ones she had joined at the athletic center, though I couldn't be sure.

Sarah raised her eyebrows as I placed my tray near her. "Hungry much?"

I rolled my eyes. "It's not mine."

As if on cue, Walter placed his tray on the opposite side of the table. But he didn't sit. Instead, he moved behind me and reached over my head to grab his food from my plate. "Thanks."

I narrowed my eyes at him as he returned to his seat. "I could have passed that to you."

He shrugged, opting to eat his grilled cheese instead of answering me. A few other guys from his dorm joined our table.

Larry placed his tray near Sarah, glancing around the table as he sat.

"So, how was everyone's first day?"

I groaned. "Okay. It's a Saturday. Why did they give us homework?"

Caroline nodded. "Not to mention, it's the first day of school."

"And it's a Saturday."

Walter shoved a forkful of salad into his mouth before pointing the empty utensil at me. "Ya se dah u weh we."

Eww. Did this boy not have any table manners? I rolled my eyes. "What?"

Apparently, no one else had understood him, since we all looked at him expectantly. Walter took his time swallowing.

"I said, *you said that already.*"

Larry shook his head. "I'm not surprised, but it feels like there's a lot."

Sarah nodded. "Yeah. But I don't think the teachers would give us anything that was too hard to do. I'm sure we'll finish it no problem. So, who wants to go to the dance tonight?"

It took me a minute to adjust to the abrupt change in subject. Sally had mentioned the dance during our form meeting and I had seen it in the *Daily Docket*.

Everyone at the table was going. Sarah looked at me expectantly.

I shrugged. "We didn't really do dances at my old school."

Larry shook his head. "This isn't a school dance. They had MAC dances while we were here over the summer. They use the stage in the MAC and there's a DJ in the corner. The MAC Attack stays open til, like, eleven."

Sarah smirked. "Well, I'm definitely in. You're coming too, Melinda."

I raised my eyebrows. "Do I have a choice?"

"No. Not really."

She was smiling, so I was pretty confident she was kidding. But I appreciated her effort to help me make new friends. Maybe I would even enjoy myself for the first time since arriving at Hartfield.

Chapter 23

THE GIRLS IN MY DORM SPENT FOREVER GETTING ready for the dance. Half an hour before it started, the floor was buzzing with the sound of people running back and forth between the showers and bathroom. Hairdryers and shouting added to the din.

As someone shouted down the hallway, I raised my eyebrows across the room at Sarah. "It sounds like they're getting ready for a formal. This is just a simple school dance, right?"

Sarah looked up from her phone and rolled her eyes. "Yeah. I don't get why everyone's freaking out." Her phone signaled several texts in rapid succession.

While she went back to her conversation, I flipped through the clothes in my closet. There was no dress code tonight. I could go in my pajamas, not that I would. But jeans would be nice. Maybe with my favorite top.

Sarah left her phone on the bed as she examined her own closet, but it chirped almost immediately. Groaning, she read the message, typed something quickly, and returned the phone to the bed. She had just enough time to pull her jeans from her closet before it chirped again.

I giggled. "Who's texting you like crazy?"

Shaking her head, she returned to her closet. "My sister. She sends, like, half an idea at a time when she texts."

"How old is she?"

"Eleven. She was telling me about her English class. I got a little lost. She either has a crush on her teacher or a boy in her class."

I was curious about her sister, but I didn't want to sound like I was being intrusive. I bit my lip. "Does she go to boarding school, too?"

"Mm-hmm. But they go home on the weekend. That's why she's texting like crazy. She's bored. Whoa. Is that the time? How'd it get so late?"

We had all agreed to meet in front of the dorms right as the dance was starting. I had about fifteen minutes to get ready. Since the mirror in my wardrobe wasn't great, I brought my hairbrush to the bathroom. As soon as I opened the door, I was hit with a deafening noise. I couldn't see through all the girls squeezed into the small space.

No dance was worth that much effort. I quickly spun around and finished getting ready in my room, warning my roommate against trying the bathroom.

When Sarah and I went downstairs, we found several of our new friends waiting for us. I tried to remember everyone's names as I followed them from the dorm. Jade, Jessie, Caroline, Xandra, and Dre.

The boys were sitting in the grass. Their names were a little harder to remember, but I knew I had met them all.

Sarah's friend Larry. His roommate Andy. The guy who ate too much, Walter. The two roommates with the woodsy names: Forrest and Leif. Two other guys from their floor whose names I kept forgetting.

We walked as a giant blob, cutting through the field to the intersection of the two main roads that cut across the campus. As we crossed, Walter shook his head beside me.

"It's like we're a gaggle."

I had no idea what he meant, but I didn't want to embarrass myself by asking. Thankfully, I was saved from showing my ignorance.

Xandra sent Walter a confused look. "What's a gaggle?"

"You know. It's a group of geese. Like a flock. It's another word for it. There's so many of us, we're like a legion, or a gaggle."

I smiled at him. "It's a funny word. But I like it. And it fits. We're a gaggle of third formers."

I liked the word so much, I promised myself not to forget it so I could add it to my vocabulary journal that night.

One of the guys whose name I couldn't remember reached the MAC first, holding the door for the rest of us. Larry clapped him on the shoulder as he passed.

"Thanks, Noah."

That was right. Once Larry said it, I remembered. I just wished I could recall everyone's names without help.

I was the last to pass through the door. As soon as I entered the lobby, I stopped so abruptly, Noah nearly crashed into me.

"Sorry."

I shook my head. "No, sorry. I didn't mean to stop short like that."

He didn't seem to mind. Smiling, he passed me to join the rest of the group. I took a moment to take in the room. It looked nothing like the last time I was here. The folding tables were gone. The room was dim. Colored lights hung above the stage, where a DJ had set up in the corner.

But the biggest change was the amount of students. They packed around the pool tables and arcade games on the left. They flooded the stage on the right. And they all appeared to be enjoying themselves.

As I followed my friends toward the stage, I glanced in the glass office. Someone had stacked the couches there. I wondered if they would be able to get them out. The door looked like it swung inward.

The students on the stage were dancing in large groups of ten to twenty people. My own gaggle was no exception. But there were smaller groups as well.

I recognized the girl in my physics class who didn't live in Woodward. She was dancing with only a couple of friends. So was my prefect. It seemed like the larger groups were probably third formers.

I had only been to two dances in my life, both at my middle school. This one was nothing like those. It reminded me of the nightclubs I saw on television shows. The deafening bass pulsed unceasingly as we danced. If there were lyrics with the music, I couldn't hear them, although I did occasionally sense when one song ended and the next began.

After dancing without stopping for close to half an hour, my throat grew dry. My roommate must have read my mind. I was just thinking how much I wanted some water when Sarah leaned close to shout in my ear.

"I'm getting a drink! Come with!"

I nodded, and Sarah leaned in the opposite direction to shout in Larry's ear. Taking my hand, she pulled me through the room to the foyer. Although I could still hear the music as I followed her downstairs, the quietness of the stairwell felt strange after spending so much time on the pulsating dance floor.

There were two vending machines at the base of the stairs. One contained snacks while the other had sodas. Using my ID, I bought a bottle of water. After Sarah got one for herself, she inclined her head toward the door beside her.

"Let's drink these down here."

I shrugged, taking a large gulp as I followed her into the lower level of the MAC. Pursing my lips, I looked around. "You know? I haven't been down here yet."

Even though I had only been at Hartfield for three days, I had learned my way around well enough that it felt odd realizing there was a building I hadn't explored.

Sarah gestured to a corridor on our left. Small doors not much bigger than my phone lined the wall. Almost directly in front of us was a service window that had been closed for the night. "That's the mail room. If you get a package, they'll email you to come pick it up at the window. But, if you think you're going to get a lot of like, real mail, you can sign up for a box."

I frowned. "Did I know that?" I felt that Sally should have told us about that during one of our many meetings this week.

Sarah giggled. "I don't know, did you? I read it in one of my orientation packets, but I can't remember if it was for the summer program or, you know, the regular one."

I hadn't read it, but my mother had taken some of my papers. With a shrug, I turned the opposite direction. Sarah led the way down a short hallway, pointing to her right as we passed.

"That's the school store. They're good in a pinch, but the mall and online are usually cheaper for school supplies."

"Like the comp books we need for English class?"

Sarah nodded. "Ooh, yeah. Thanks for reminding me. I'll order those first thing tomorrow. I wonder if I could get same-day delivery for those."

She didn't seem to be looking for an answer, continuing to a small room at the end of the hall. As soon as she crossed the threshold, the lights switched on. Sarah pointed to the glass wall on the opposite side of the room.

"That's the pool. You can't really see it right now, but it's pretty big. Eight lanes, I think. I used it a couple times over the summer."

The room had a couple of couches, but we didn't stay long enough to sit in them. We both downed the rest of our waters, tossing the bottles in the recycling bins beside the school store before going back upstairs.

After spending so much time in the quiet lower level, the blast of noise startled me when passed through the foyer. It didn't seem to bother Sarah, though, who crossed to the dance floor quickly. Our friends hadn't moved, although their circle had tightened slightly.

I inserted myself between Dre and Jade, losing myself in the music. I heard a minute change in the rhythm, and Jade leaned close to shout in my ear.

"I love this song!"

How could she tell? It sounded just like all the rest. But Jade had already turned back to the circle.

Despite the deafening noise, I had a lot of fun dancing with my new friends. A little after eleven, the MAC lights grew brighter until they were full blast. The music slowly died, and the DJ said something I couldn't understand.

My friends and I had danced our way into the corner furthest from the main entrance. Instead of fighting her way to the exit, Sarah sat on the floor right where she was. With a shrug, I joined her. Most of our friends did as well.

Jade was beaming. "That was so much fun! So much better than my last school."

I nodded. "I know. My old school? We had dances for each grade. Like, only the sixth grade could go to the sixth-grade dance."

Walter frowned. "That doesn't sound very fun."

I shook my head. "Oh, it gets better. So the first one was at, like, the end of September or something. Only, like, a quarter of my class even went. We spent most of the time standing on the side of the room. And the music was nothing like this."

"No?"

"Nope. Mostly like pop stuff you hear on the radio. Although the DJ did throw in some line dances that almost no one did. I mean, I think we even did the Hokey Pokey."

Walter raised his eyebrows. "Sounds really lame."

I nodded. "Yeah. Pretty much. There was one slow song and only one couple danced to it. And everyone else teased them about it for weeks, even after they broke up. So then, a couple months later, the student council or whoever tried again. The night was cut short when someone set off a stink bomb."

Some of my friends laughed, but Jade gasped. "Oh no! What happened?"

189

"We had to evacuate the gym. We called our parents from the cafeteria and they picked us up early. After that, some of the other grades had dances, but we never did."

Sarah jerked her head toward the exit. "Looks like the line died down."

As I followed my friends back to the dorm, I thought about the story I had just shared. Had Brittany and Casey attended a dance their first week of school? I didn't think so. I had still been home. They would have mentioned it.

And, even if there *had* been a dance, would it have been as fun as this one had been? Something made me think the answer was no.

Hartfield was nothing like what I had been expecting high school to be. But maybe that wasn't such a bad thing after all?

Chapter 24

SUNDAY MORNING, A DEAFENING NOISE AWOKE ME from a sound sleep. In my dreamlike state, I thought an ambulance was driving through the hallway. Sarah beat me to the door. When she opened it, the noise grew even louder. I looked out beside her. Half the girls on our floor were peeking out of their rooms.

Adrienne was shouting over the noise. "This is a fire drill. Get out to the field as quickly as possible. This is a fire drill."

I quickly ducked back into my room. I didn't want to go outside barefoot. I slipped on my shower shoes. Seeing me, Sarah did the same, and we both joined the tide of girls leaving the building.

When we got to the ball field in front of our dorm, Sarah and I huddled together with some of our friends. The air was chillier than I had expected, and I got the impression many of the girls from the dorm felt the same. Most of us were rubbing our bare arms to keep warm. Nearly all of us were in our pajamas and only a few had thought to grab shoes.

No one made much noise. The only conversations I heard were girls threatening that this had better be an actual emergency because they were so tired.

We weren't on the field long before Sally and Clarissa emerged from the dorm. The dean smiled, speaking loudly enough for all to hear.

"That wasn't so bad for your first drill."

Clarissa nodded. "There's still plenty of room for improvement, however."

The pair droned on for a few minutes, but I paid little attention. Something about monthly drills and decreasing our evacuation times. I wondered if anyone was listening. All the girls near me had glazed looks on their faces.

Eventually, Sally allowed us to return to our rooms. I heard a lot of mutterings about going back to bed. But I was wide awake. It was late enough that there was no possibility of me falling back asleep, especially after spending ten minutes in the crisp morning air.

I turned to my Sarah as we entered our room. "You going back to sleep?"

"Nah. I'm wide awake."

I looked around. "We should clean the room."

"Oh! Good idea!"

It wasn't that messy. Sarah and I made our beds and organized the books on our desks. I straightened the shoes under my bed while Sarah swept the floor with the broom she had tucked between her wardrobe and the wall.

We finished cleaning in ten minutes. Flopping onto our beds, Sarah frowned at me.

"Okay. Now what?"

My stomach rumbled in response.

Sarah giggled. "Okay. Breakfast it is."

By the time we showered and dressed, the dining hall was open. Since it was still fairly early on a Sunday morning, I expected us to be the only people there. But there were a smattering of other students in the main section of the dining hall, as well as a couple of families with young children in the smaller area. As I entered the servery, I glanced at the senior section to see two boys and a girl in special dress outfits. At first, I wondered if there was a senior party, but I quickly realized they were most likely heading to church.

I was in the mood for pancakes. After piling a few on my plate and drowning them in syrup, I grabbed a glass of orange juice and searched for my roommate. She was waiting for a server behind the counter to make her a waffle.

She smiled as I approached her. "You go ahead. I'll find you."

With a shrug, I headed to what I had started to think of as our usual table. I was nearly there when I heard my name.

"Hey. Melinda. Over here!"

I turned in all directions. It took a moment to see someone waving to me from the other side of the columns. I continued to the back of the dining hall, using the rear arch to enter the smaller section and join Larry and Walter at their table.

They couldn't have been there long, since their trays were so overburdened. They each had a stack of pancakes and a second plate with scrambled eggs, as well as two glasses of juice. Walter also had a waffle. I shook my head as I sat across from them.

Walter shoved some eggs into his mouth before pointing at me with his fork. "You're up early."

I shrugged. "We had a fire drill this morning. Sarah and I decided we couldn't go back to sleep, so we figured we'd get some food."

Larry nodded as Sarah joined us. "Yeah, us too. Couldn't go back to sleep. I was going to go for a run, but Walter here mentioned breakfast and my stomach won out."

Sarah pointed to Larry's tray. "You might need to go running after a breakfast like that."

Larry examined his plate with a puzzled expression. "What's wrong with my breakfast?"

I couldn't help but laugh. Sarah smiled. "So, what are your plans for our one-day weekend?"

"Hum-bock." Walter's mouth was so full he looked like a squirrel gathering nuts for the winter. We all stared at him, waiting for him to swallow and take a sip of his juice before translating for us.

"Homework. I have a lot of homework to do. I figure I'll start it now and try to get at least half done by lunchtime." He shoved a smaller forkful of food into this mouth. "Then I'll go to the MAC after lunch and catch the game before finishing work."

Larry shook his head. "Well, I'm not wasting a Sunday. I'm going to go down to the MAC and see if I can't get some cartoons."

I wanted to laugh at his joke. But he wasn't kidding. I raised my eyebrows in his direction. "Aren't you a little old for cartoons?"

He smiled. "You're never too old for cartoons. Wanna come?"

"I think I'll get a head start on my homework."

But my roommate seemed to like the idea. "I'll go! I haven't watched morning cartoons in a while. It sounds fun."

Larry and Sarah fell into an intense discussion about their favorite animated shows, both what they watched when they were younger and what they enjoyed now. They didn't seem to notice that Walter and I weren't part of the conversation. The longer they talked, the more uncomfortable I grew. I wanted to say something to Walter, just to break the silence, but I didn't know what to say. The only topic that came to my mind was the schoolwork waiting for me in my room.

"So, do you have a lot of homework? I mean, I know you said you had a lot. But is it a lot because it's hard or because it's just, well, a lot?"

I could feel my cheeks growing warm. Could my question be more lame? Walter was probably laughing at me on the inside.

He sent me an odd, thoughtful glance as he drained one of his juice glasses. I couldn't read his look. Was he wondering why I had asked that question? Was he trying to figure out if I was serious? Was he debating whether to answer me or ignore me?

After what felt like forever, Walter returned the glass to his tray. "You know? I never really thought about that. It just felt like a lot of homework. But, if you think about it, I guess the amount isn't really all that bad. Let's see."

He stared into space, ticking each subject on his fingers. "My physics teacher just wants us to read a chapter. That sounds like a lot, but when you figure at least half that chapter is pictures, which I just ignore, and some side stories, which I also ignore, it's probably only like ten pages of actual reading so that's not so bad."

He was probably right, but it felt like a lot.

"My math teacher wants us to do twenty problems. Again, not too many, but it looked hard, so I just don't want to do it. What else? English. We have to read a Greek myth. I don't think it's that long, but I suspect it will feel like I'm reading a hundred pages before I'm done with it. Latin, we only have to translate a few lines, so that'll be easy."

I sent him a confused look. "You're in Latin, too?"

He nodded. "Yeah, first year. I'm in your class. You were kind of daydreaming when I came in, so I'm not surprised you didn't notice. I was going to say hi, but Mr. Henderson followed me into the room, so I didn't get a chance."

I couldn't believe I had ignored one of the few people I knew in my classes. I shook my head mournfully. "I'm sorry. I wasn't trying to be rude or anything. I was a little out of it. By Latin, I was so overwhelmed with the rest of my day that I really had no idea what was going on."

"It's okay. I had physics, math, and English before Latin. By the time Mr. Henderson assigned that homework, I thought I would scream. I mean, seriously, homework on the *first* day of school? And a Saturday, at that?"

I gave a small smile. Hadn't I been saying the same thing yesterday?

Walter nodded at me. "What about you? What's your homework like?"

I shrugged, trying to remember my classes. "I have to draw something for art. Like, that's the assignment. *Draw something.* I haven't decided what yet. Then I had physics, Latin, math, and English and my homework sounds like the same as yours. But, hang on." I frowned. Something wasn't adding up. "Physics, math, English, Latin. Are you only taking four classes?"

Walter groaned. "Nah. I've got a programming class at the end of the day. I've got to read a bunch for that, too. Forgot about that one."

I gave a small laugh. "I don't blame you. My brain more or less of shut off during Latin."

"Yeah, mine, too. Hey. Wasn't it funny when Mr. Henderson sat down? I mean, I saw him walking over to the desk, and I was thinking to myself, *How is this gargantuan man going to fit in such a tiny desk?* And then, he was able to do it!"

I closed my eyes with a sigh. I was getting so frustrated with everyone around me using words I couldn't understand. Even though I didn't like Walter thinking I was ignorant, I wanted to follow the conversation.

Frowning, I opened my eyes. "What does *gargantuan* mean?"

Thankfully, Walter's expression suggested he didn't think less of me for not knowing the term. "Um ... giant. Tremendous. Henderson's so tall, it's the perfect word to describe him."

I nodded. I could see that. But I wasn't sure what else to say. As Walter and I finished the last few bites of our breakfasts, I got uncomfortable again. He would probably think I was a geek, but school was the only topic that would come to my mind.

"You know, I have never felt so overwhelmed with homework before. I mean, school has always been so easy."

Walter nodded. "I was just thinking that! I used to help my friends with their homework, since they had trouble with it. We used to hang out at the library after classes."

He cut himself off, his face turning the color of a tomato. Was he embarrassed about spending his free time in the library? That wasn't so ridiculous.

I sent him a sympathetic smile. "You know? I used to volunteer at my local library. I had spent so much time there that the librarian offered me a job one day. I re-shelved books in the children's section. They didn't pay me or anything, but I didn't care. It was fun. And after I finished, I would go upstairs to the adult library and read in one of the reading nooks until my mom picked me up."

Walter smiled, his face turning back to normal. "See? That's the great thing about this place. In my old school, someone probably would have beaten me up if anyone found out I spent free time in the library. Here, though, everyone is so cerebral that things like that are normal."

I raised an eyebrow. "*Cerebral*? Does that mean smart or something?"

As Walter nodded, Sarah and Larry stood. My roommate turned to me. "We're heading over to the MAC. You sure you don't want to come?"

I nodded. "Positive."

Larry turned to Walter. "Bro? We're gonna try to find *DragonWorld*."

Walter shook his head. "Definitely not."

With a shrug, Larry and Sarah grabbed their trays and headed to the dish room. I wanted to follow them, but Walter and I were alone at the table. Was it acceptable for me to just leave? Was I supposed to say something to Walter first?

He looked just as uncomfortable as I felt. Eventually, he slowly got to his feet. "I guess I better get started on that homework if I want to catch the game later."

I immediately stood and grabbed my tray. "I was just thinking that." As he followed me to the dish room, I frowned. "Well, that I wanted to start my homework. No, not start it. Just look at it. I don't want to do it. I just want to look at it, so I feel less worried about it."

Walter nodded. "Yeah. That's what I'm feeling. I don't really want to do it. I just want it to be done so I can worry about something else."

As we walked back to the dorms, I decided it wouldn't hurt to keep talking about our classes. "So, your homework sounded a lot like mine. Who do you have for physics?"

"Mr. Smith. He's one of my advisors. How about you?"

"Mr. Wilson."

"What about math? Are you in geometry, too?"

I nodded. "Yeah. I have Mr. Davidson. He's the first person I ever met who has a pocket protector."

Walter chuckled. "I have him, too. When I saw that, it took every ounce of energy not to laugh. I mean, quintessential dork, right?"

I bit my lip. "I don't know. Quin-what?"

"*Quintessential.*" He frowned a moment. "Uh, stereotypical?"

"Oh. Yeah. That was more or less what I was thinking."

"Who do you have for English? I have Mr. Johnson."

"Me too."

Walter stopped in front of his dorm, turning to me. "Look. Since we have the same homework tonight, you wanna study together in the library? Might make it a little less painful."

I didn't reply right away. He had a point. Studying together would probably be better than working alone. But would it be too weird to study with someone I didn't really know?

He must have seen my hesitation. "I just don't want to study alone. I have this fear that if I go back to my room, I'll fall asleep or play video games or something and not get anything done. It'll only be until lunchtime. After lunch, I'm going to watch the game, remember?"

It probably wouldn't hurt to study with him. I sighed. "Yeah. That's probably not a bad idea."

"Great. I'll meet you here in a few minutes."

Nodding, I watched him jog up the stairs to his dorm before heading to my own. As I made my way to my room, I thought about all the times I had studied with friends in the library. Was it possible I had just made a new friend?

Chapter 25

I STARED AT MY DESK, WONDERING WHAT I SHOULD bring to the library. Would all these books even fit in my bag? I opened my assignment pad to the page where I had written all my homework. I probably didn't need every book on my desk.

I packed my physics and Latin textbooks, but opted to leave the workbooks behind. I grabbed my math text and the book of Greek myths. After rummaging through my drawer, I found my package of looseleaf paper and added that to my bag. Lastly, I threw in my assignment pad, my completed homework folder, and my calculator.

My gaze fell on my vocabulary journal. Walter had taught me several unfamiliar words in the past twelve or so hours. After scribbling them and their definitions into the book, I added the journal to my bag. I had a feeling I would be entering more words to it before I was done studying. After checking for all my writing instruments, I tossed my phone and charger into the front pocket and shouldered my bag.

It was beyond heavy. Would I have to do this every night? As I made my way downstairs, I shook my head. No. Only when I studied in the library.

Walter was waiting for me, and I felt a little better seeing his bag looked as heavy as mine. Despite my early start this morning, we had dawdled long enough that I saw more people milling about the campus as we trudged across the street.

I followed Walter through main entrance of the library. It didn't look like much. We were in a small, round foyer. To my left was a door leading to the covered bridge to the dining hall. To my right was a tall staircase. In front of me was a set of double glass doors.

Walter pointed at them. "That's the quiet study area. Someone told me there are places we can study together, but I'm not sure where they are."

I shrugged. "I'm sure we'll find them."

He opened the door, gesturing for me to lead the way. I marched to the center of the room before turning in a slow circle. I could not believe this was my school library.

The room had to be two stories tall, with floor-to-ceiling bookshelves lining the walls. The books resting on them looked as old as the school. Between the bookcases were windows bigger than me. Small desks sat before them. Not the study tables I had seen in my old school library. These were antique desks.

Throughout the room sat couches of various sizes, some between bookcases, other arranged in small conversational groupings. Along the back wall sat a stone fireplace with more couches before it and a doorway to the right that I thought might lead to the librarian's offices. Through it, I could see books on display.

My old school library, not to mention the public one, had computers and current books. Walter thought this one had an area where we could study together. There had to be more to this library. But how did we get there?

A large circulation desk sat just beside the entrance. Behind it sat a little woman who was the stereotypical librarian. Her gray hair was pulled into a tight bun on the back of her head. She wore small wire-rimmed glasses on a chain. She was staring at us with a look that simultaneously said *welcome* and *you better not be here to cause any trouble.*

Biting my lip, I approached her hesitantly, keeping my voice low. "Um, is there a place we can go study? Like, without having to whisper?"

The librarian looked annoyed that I had bothered her. She pointed to the doorway beside the fireplace. "There are study rooms upstairs."

She didn't actually explain how to *get* there, but I was too intimidated to ask. Walter and I were smart. We could probably figure it out. Nodding in thanks, I led the way into the corridor.

It wasn't long and turned abruptly nearly as soon as we entered, dumping us into the modern section of the library. In front of us was a bank of computers. A room to the left had rows and rows of bookcases. To the right was a set of doors leading outside. On one side was a second circulation desk, while on the other was the entrance to a stairwell.

I pointed to it. "I'm going to guess that's how we get to the upstairs study rooms?"

"You think?"

I pretended to sneer, but he missed my expression as he led the way. Because the first floor was so tall, it felt like we were going upstairs forever. But eventually, we reached the top and found ourselves in another corridor.

I shook my head. "I feel like we're in a maze. Why does this have to be so complicated?"

Walter shrugged. "It's like they don't *want* people studying up here."

The hallway ended in a common room with the entrances to several study areas. Some had solid walls. Others had glass, allowing us to peer into the room easily. Walter and I examined each one. Although all the areas had study tables, some also had couches or overstuffed chairs. One room even had a fireplace.

After peeking through each door, Walter pointed to a room. There was a small window on one side that looked into the hallway and through the glass wall of the study area across the way. On the opposite side was a bank of windows looking over the campus. I could see the humanities building and part of Walter's dorm.

In the middle of the room was a study table for four. As Walter and I settled on opposite sides of it, I cast a longing glance at the two oversized chairs in the corner.

"I better not sit there. I'll probably fall asleep."

Walter nodded. "Tell me about it. So, what should we work on first?"

I removed my assignment pad from my bag, opening it to tonight's homework. We didn't have any written work for either physics or English. I frowned. "I don't really feel like reading yet. How about Latin?"

Walter had unpacked all his books on the table beside him. I did the same before pulling out some looseleaf and a pen.

Removing my Latin book from the stack, I opened to the assigned page.

Walter read the story aloud, and I tried to follow along. However, since I had never taken Latin before, I spent most of the time glancing at the glossary at the bottom of the page.

The passage was short. When Walter finished, he glanced at me. "Okay. So, I know it's not part of the assignment, but I think we should translate this before we answer the questions."

I nodded. Not only did I like that idea, I even wrote out the translation as we went. Hopefully that would help when we tried to answer the questions.

Walter read the first one. "Number one. What is the name of Cornelia's father?"

I knew the answer, but I wasn't sure how to write it. "Do we need to write these in complete sentences? And do they have to be in Latin?"

Walter screwed up his face as he read his syllabus. "Henderson didn't say. I don't think we learned how to write complete sentences in Latin, though."

He was right. Erring on the side of caution, I opted for complete sentences in English. "Cornelia's father is Cornelius." After Walter wrote the same, I read the next question. "What is Cornelia doing?"

Walter pointed to the line in his book. "Cornelia scribit."

I glanced at the bottom of the page as I slowly wrote my answer. "Cornelia is writing."

Ten questions and nearly an hour later, I slid both my assignment and translation into my completed homework folder.

"Hey, let's do math next."

I glanced at Walter, who was holding my assignment pad. As he returned it to the table, he pointed to the words I had scribbled at the bottom of the page yesterday. "What's that?"

As I pulled my vocabulary journal from my bag, I could feel my cheeks growing warm. But I passed it to him anyway, doing my best to explain as he flipped through a few pages.

"I have a vocabulary journal. Whenever there's a word I don't know, I write it down and look it up later. Those are the words I heard yesterday that I meant to look up. I'll do it later."

Shrugging, he returned the journal. "You don't have to. I'll help you out. A *syllabus* is—well, aren't you going to write this down?"

Was he serious? He seemed to be. His smile suggested he wanted to help me, not that he thought less of me for not knowing these words.

I flipped through my journal to my last entry and wrote *syllabus* on the next line before looking at him expectantly.

"A syllabus is basically an outline for the term. Most teachers use it to list all our assignments. But not all of them. My programming teacher just gave us a list of topics. I think she's going to base our homework on how well each class goes."

I nodded. I had more or less guessed that was the definition. After Walter helped me to understand all the words I had written yesterday, he opened his math book to the assigned page.

I left my journal on the chair beside me as I grabbed a fresh sheet of paper. When I finished working through the first problem, Walter frowned at his page.

"What'd you get for number one?"

I glanced at the answer I had just circled. "Eighteen."

With a harrumph, Walter erased his work. At first, I thought he would just write my answer, but out of the corner of my eye, I saw him calculate the problem again. Every so often, he would glance at my page. That was probably the reason I finished first.

Before I could stow the paper in my folder, Walter took it from me.

I reached for it. "Hey!"

He waved me away, laying my paper beside his own. I watched as he examined both pages. Every few problems, he would erase something on his paper and fix his answer.

Shaking my head, I opened my physics book, then notebook, writing the chapter title at the top of the page. Before I could read the first sentence, however, Walter returned my paper, slamming his book closed and checking his phone.

"Lunchtime!"

I sighed, glancing at the table. The books beside me were for the assignments I had yet to complete. The ones on the chair were for the subjects that were done. Walter's side looked a lot like mine.

I frowned. "I don't want to pack all this stuff and lug it downstairs, just to bring it back up here and unpack it all again."

Walter snapped his fingers, pointing at me. "That's a good point. I'll be right back."

He grabbed his phone and rushed out of the room. Was he going to the dining hall without me? After spending the last couple of hours together, I had assumed we would eat lunch together.

No. He said he'd be right back. He probably ran to the bathroom or something. I would give him a few minutes before going to the dining hall.

I glanced at my physics book, but Walter had put the idea of food in my head. Studying wasn't going to happen for a while. I walked to the window, gazing at the students moving about the campus in small groups. Some were making their way toward the dining hall, others were heading in the direction of the MAC. All the students I saw seemed to be with at least one other person. Everyone on campus had made friends. No one was alone.

When my phone played an unfamiliar song, I turned to the table. I thought I had silenced it when I had entered the library. And where did that ring tone come from?

I frowned at the phone in my hands. It wasn't mine. When I recognized the number on the screen, I realized what must have happened.

I swiped to answer. "Hello?"

"Melinda?" I recognized Walter's voice immediately. "Good. You answered. I was worried you wouldn't. Come on down to the front entrance. You can leave your stuff. Oh, but bring my phone."

Walter ended the call before I could respond. I glanced around the room. I didn't mind leaving my books, but for some reason, the thought of not having my vocabulary journal made me uncomfortable. I tossed it into my backpack, grabbed Walter's phone, and followed the maze back to the quiet study area.

Walter was waiting for me in the vestibule. When I passed him his phone, he returned mine with a smirk.

"Thanks. I added myself to your contacts."

"Okay?"

While Walter led the way to the dining hall, I considered what he had said. My contacts list was small for a reason. I didn't like scrolling through a ton of numbers when I wanted to get in touch with a friend.

But I had spent my morning doing schoolwork with Walter. We seemed to get along well enough. As I entered the dining hall, I came to a sudden realization.

I had made a new friend.

Chapter 26

STUDENTS PACKED THE DINING HALL. EVERY TABLE in the senior section was filled, most holding more people than chairs. The sixth formers were chatting animatedly as they ate and everyone seemed to be enjoying their day off.

I lost Walter in the servery. After doing a quick tour, I realized nothing sounded appealing. What I really wanted was a sandwich. I took my tray to the sandwich bar, pleased to see there was no line.

The server smiled at me. "What can I get for you?"

"Uh, turkey and provolone sandwich on a roll, please?"

Nodding, the woman made my sandwich expertly, passing me the plate over the plastic sneeze guard. After thanking her, I brought my tray to the toppings bar to lather my sandwich with mustard and mayonnaise. When I went to get a soda from the beverage island, I saw someone exiting with a plate of fries. Those would complement my sandwich perfectly.

I found them near the chicken patties. I also found Walter. He held a plate toward me.

"Hey. Think you can help me?"

Rolling my eyes, I took his chicken patty and fries, following him to our usual table. Sarah and Larry were both there, along with about half a dozen people from our dorms. As I settled beside my roommate, I mentally reviewed everyone's names. Sarah. Larry. Walter, who was taking his food from my plate before I could pass it to him. Forrest. Jade. Leif. Andy and Dre, who were bickering worse than me and my brother.

I had been eating most of my meals with these people. Didn't that mean they were my friends, too?

I passed Sarah my phone. "I need your number so I can text you when I get lost."

Giggling, she entered the number, taking a selfie for her profile picture and texting herself before returning the phone. I handed it to Dre on my other side.

"I want everyone's numbers. So we can meet for meals and stuff."

Sarah nodded. "Yeah, me, too."

As we ate, we passed our phones around the table. I typed my own number so many times, my thumbs hurt. But at the end of the meal, my contact list was full of my new friends.

After all the phones had been returned to their owners, my friends took turns sharing how they had spent the morning. I worried they would tease me for starting my homework so early, but no one did. If anything, my comments seemed to remind everyone they had work to do as well.

Most of my friends had been eating for a while, so I wasn't at the table long before they started to leave. By the time I finished eating, only Sarah, Larry, and Walter remained. Since I didn't want to be in the library until the middle of the night, I collected my things onto my tray and stood, giving a small wave to the table.

"I'm heading back to the library. Later."

I was about to enter the dish room when I heard Walter calling me. "Melinda. Wait up."

Turning, I saw him following me. After we deposited our trays, we walked back to the library together. I waited until we were through the senior section before turning to him.

"You going to stay? Or are you going to go watch football?"

Walter frowned. "If I watch the game, I'll have a lot of work to do later. But if I do my homework, I'll miss the game."

Walter continued debating with himself all the way back to the study room. I couldn't help but giggle. His arguments were hilarious.

He cocked his head to one side. "Two strong teams. It should be a good game."

Frowning, he leaned his head in the opposite direction. "But then I'll be up all night doing my homework. And it's a lot of homework. All that reading will probably put me to sleep."

He snapped his fingers. "Maybe I could watch the game and leave at halftime to finish my homework."

He shook his head. "I'll never leave. I'll want to see the second half. But maybe I could do one more subject, then watch the second half."

He groaned. "Then I'll probably be up all night doing homework again."

I offered no opinion, since he obviously wasn't looking for any. As soon as we entered our study room, Walter stared at his pile of books and gave a mournful sigh.

"There's no way I'll finish all this if I watch the game. I'll catch the highlights online tonight."

Our physics assignment took a long time to complete. We traded off reading aloud, but I needed Walter to help me understand each paragraph. When we finally finished, he glanced around.

"I need a study break."

I raised my eyebrows. "You going to go watch football?"

"Nah. But I was thinking of going for a walk. Wanna explore the rest of the library?"

I shrugged. "Why not?"

We had already seen the entire second floor. Other than a single occupant restroom, it was all study rooms. We took the stairs all the way to the lower level, emerging into a forest of bookshelves. As we wandered through them, I pointed to the sign on one of the end caps.

"Are those call numbers? Because I don't remember letters in the Dewey decimal system."

Walter frowned. "Hang on. I know this. It's . . . oh! Library of Congress system."

I raised my eyebrows. "Like that place in, where is it? DC, I think? Where they keep all the books ever published?"

Walter nodded. "Yeah. But a lot of colleges use the classification system, too."

"Why?"

He shrugged. "No clue."

"How do you even know about it?"

"I remember reading something about it recently." I wanted to know more, but he was turning the color of a tomato, so I let the subject drop.

The basement was large and seemed to hold the library's entire collection of books. Walter and I discovered a second staircase in the back corner. When we climbed it, we found ourselves in the small room I had seen from the corridor this morning. Glancing at these books, I realized this was the reference section. Besides the bookshelves, there were some single-person study tables. Unlike this morning, a few of them were now occupied.

Our tour completed, Walter and I returned to the study room and I pointed at the overstuffed leather chairs in the corner.

"I wanna sit there to read."

Walter shrugged. "Okay." Grabbing his book of myths, he settled into one of them with a groan. "Yeah. I'm going to fall asleep if I stay here."

"Why don't we read aloud?" I sank into the chair opposite him.

Walter smirked. "If you read to me, I'm going to fall asleep."

"Nah. We'll take turns."

"Okay. Let's try it."

Although switching paragraphs made the assignment take longer, I enjoyed reading the story with Walter. By the time we finished, the dining hall was open.

Glad to have completed most of our assignments, Walter and I returned all our books to our bags. As we headed down the stairs, Walter turned to me.

"So, do we go back to the dorm, drop off these backbreaking things, and get everyone for supper? Or just forget them and go eat?"

Shaking my head, I held up my phone. "I have a better idea."

I created a new group text to invite all my Hartfield friends to dinner. A moment later, Walter's phone chirped. He laughed at the readout.

"Yeah. I guess I'll join you for supper."

We left our bags at our usual table before heading to the servery. While it wasn't packed, there were certainly many people getting their dinners. Tonight's hot entrée was stir-fry with rice. I was in the mood to try something new. I even offered to take Walter's back to the table while he went in search of more food.

As I settled into my seat, I checked my phone. Not only did my friends respond that they were on their way, they were bringing floor mates whose numbers I had yet to collect. Before long, my friends had stolen chairs from neighboring tables and turned their trays in order to make camp at what had become *our* table.

As we again passed around our phones to get everyone's numbers, I looked around, counting my new friends. Walter. Sarah. Larry. Andy. Dre. Xandra. Forrest. Leif. Jade. Jessi. Pete. Noah. Caroline. I had met these people only a few days ago, yet I felt closer to them than I had ever been with Brittany and Casey. I still loved my friends from home, but their lives had already changed so dramatically without me.

When my parents first told me about Hartfield three months ago, I thought I would never be happy here. But as I looked around the table, I couldn't imagine living without these people.

I pulled out my phone and added the rest of the names to my group text. Before closing it, I gave the group a name: *My Hartfield Family.*

I had found my new home.

Melinda's Vocabulary Journal

- academic integrity: adhering to the code of values regarding schoolwork (return to story)
- anthology: A collection of literary works, such as stories or poems (return to story)
- arduous: difficult or strenuous (return to story)
- campus: the grounds and buildings that make up a school (return to story)
- cerebral: Intellectual, smart (return to story)
- co-educational (co-ed): 'boys and girls' (return to story)
- commencement: the end; graduation (return to story)
- common room: large living room (return to story)
- comprise: being made up of (return to story)
- convocation: a special ceremony to start the school year (return to story)
- day student: a student who does not live at a boarding school but commutes there daily (return to story)
- dean: principal (return to story)
- dormitory (dorm): a building where students live and sleep; the bedroom building (return to story)
- edifice: building (return to story)
- form: grade (as in 9th, 10th, 11th, 12th) (return to story)
- gaggle: A group of geese; a flock (return to story)
- gargantuan: Giant, tremendous (return to story)
- headmaster: the head of the school (return to story)
- humanities: branches of learning that include English, history, religion, and philosophy (return to story)
- immunization: vaccine given to prevent illness (return to story)
- interminable: seemingly endless (return to story)
- interscholastic: competing against other schools (return to story)
- intramural: a sport that does not compete (return to story)
- legion: A great number, a multitude (return to story)

- matriculation ceremony: a special ceremony to start the school year (return to story)
- office hours: a period of time when the teacher is in the office and available for a student to just drop in and ask questions (return to story)
- orientation: a meeting introducing people to the school and its rules (return to story)
- P.G.: post-graduate. a person who has graduated high school but continues to take high school classes (return to story)
- plagiarism: presenting someone else's work (ideas or words) as one's own (return to story)
- portfolio: suitcase (return to story)
- prefect: an older student, usually a sixth-former, who is in charge of younger students (return to story)
- prestigious: fancy, popular (return to story)
- quintessential: perfectly representing something (return to story)
- rotunda: round room (return to story)
- score: twenty (return to story)
- syllabus: an outline, usually for a class (return to story)
- vape pen: an electronic device used to inhale vapors (return to story)

It's not over yet!

Read more about Melinda's adventures at Hartfield in

Adjusting to a New Life
The first book in the Hartfield Chronicles Series

**Melinda knew adjusting to high school would be difficult.
But will she flunk out before she even has a chance?**

Two hours away from home, Melinda quickly learns that her new boarding school is much more challenging than her public middle school. Her new friends and teacher must become her family.
But Melinda never expected the assignments to be *this* difficult. How will she have time to make new friends if she's constantly studying?
And then there's the boys. For the first time in her life, she has a boyfriend.

When an old friend re-enters her life, she must learn how to balance school with her social life if she wants to succeed at Hartfield.

When you finish reading Melinda's story,
flip the book over to read Pat's story.

Patrick McGregor is one of the most recognized faces in Hollywood. But sometimes, he just wants to be a normal sixteen-year-old.

Pat thought missing the beginning of the school year to film a new movie on location in Hawaii sounded ideal. But, for the first time in his life, his family isn't around to keep him company. A demanding film schedule and lackadaisical tutor don't help combat the homesickness.

When a family member falls ill, Pat must examine the true meaning of family.

Read now at
https://books2read.com/Lesson1

**Can't get enough of Melinda's life in boarding school?
Read more in Hartfield Chronicles**

Hartfield Chronicles is an ongoing webserial that follows the lives of Melinda and her friends as they navigate their way through boarding school. Each episode features two stories: one from Melinda's point of view and one from Pat's, along with an excerpt from Melinda's writing journal.

Read for free at
www.hartfieldchronicles.com

Did you like this story? Want to learn about other new releases?
Join my newsletter at
https://ashleighstevens.eo.page/yanewsletter

As a thank you, you'll receive a FREE copy of

Camp Piquaqua

INDEPENDENT PUBLISHERS
OF NEW ENGLAND
2021 BOOK AWARD FINALIST

Ana has the perfect job.
Unfortunately, it means working with TJ.

We quickly huddled together, burying our heads under our bags. I lost track of time under the table with TJ's arm around me, shielding me from the storm. I was surprised that this annoying creature could make me feel so safe. I squeezed my eyes shut as a barrage of unfamiliar noises assaulted my ears and wondered whether I would ever open them again.

Seventeen-year-old Ana cannot wait for summer, when she gets to co-lead the overnight hikes at her uncle's family camp. Sure, it means working with his brother-in-law, TJ, a boy her age whom she cannot stand. But, she is willing to put aside their differences in order to have a fantastic summer. When tragedy strikes, Ana and TJ must work together, with the help of the legendary piquaqua bird, to help restore the camp in time for summer.

Elephant on my Chest

He's the vile boy next door.
Who also knows her biggest secret.

Sixteen-year-old Izzy is excited about the all-school ski trip. She is looking forward to learning to ski, even if she will be the only one on the bunny hill. Of course, she has to first make it through a five-hour bus ride with the vilest—albeit cutest—boy in school. And survive the roommates who keep breaking her one rule: "No sleeping with your boyfriend in my bed!"

When an unexpected power outage triggers a panic attack, Izzy is forced to tell Pug her biggest secret. She's even more surprised to learn his, spending the rest of the long weekend looking at her enemy in a new light.

But their secrets are nothing compared to the one Izzy's mother has been keeping for sixteen years. When Izzy discovers the truth, she must learn to confront her panic disorder or else live with the elephant sitting on her chest.

Warning: This book describes panic attacks. If this will trigger you, this book may not be for you.

Read now at
https://books2read.com/Elephant

About the Author

Once upon a time, there was a girl who loved reading and learning so much that she wanted to share her writing with others. She wrote her first novella at twelve-years-old, although it has never been published. She continued writing for the next twenty years, developing a writing style and finding a comfortable genre.

In 2010, just before the birth of her first child, Ashleigh decided to publish her first novel. Not long after, Ashleigh decided to become a stay-at-home mother in order to spend time with her daughter and continue her writing.

Currently, Ashleigh lives in Southern Connecticut with her husband and her four beautiful children, whom she homeschools. In her spare time, Ashleigh continues working on her novels, hoping to publish more soon.

Read more at www.AshleighStevensBSB.com

Other Works by Ashleigh Stevens

Young Adults
Camp Piquaqua
Elephant on my Chest

Hartfield Chronicles
Lesson 0: A New Home
Lesson 1: Adjusting to a New Life
Webserial

Romances
Kayaks, Kisses & Monsters
Mooncrossed

Mysteries
(writing as Carrie Latimer)
One Night In Sedona

To receive updates on new releases, visit
www.AshleighsStevensBSB.com
or join my newsletter
https://ashleighstevens.eo.page/yanewsletter

www.ingramcontent.com/pod-product-compliance
Lightning Source LLC
Chambersburg PA
CBHW020406180626
46812CB00003B/861